THE MAGIC WITHIN

TRIPLE QUEST

Book 2

Lee Marsh

This is a 2nd edition re-write of
The Magic Within – Triple Quest
2017

ISBN: 9781521291849

For Lorraine with love

Copyright 2017 Lee Marsh
All rights reserved

The author hereby asserts her moral right to be identified as the author of the work

All rights reserved. No part of this publication may be reproduced, stored in a retrieval system, or transmitted, in any form, or by any means, electronic, mechanical, photocopying, recording or otherwise, without the prior permission of the copyright holder

Chapter 1

'Daaddd!'

The loud cry escaped Rosie's lips as she plopped back into her body. Bella, Rosie's little dog and faithful companion, jumped up from where she had been lying at the foot of Rosie's chair, and barked, just the once, but it was heart felt.

All had been peaceful at the homestead before Rosie had screamed, which made it sound even louder.

Hector, the pony had settled himself in his stable after enjoying his supper, and was now munching on some nice fresh hay hanging up in a hay-net ready for when he felt peckish later, but he had decided to sample a little now. Startled by the sudden cry, his head shot up in the air, his eyes opened wide, and a loud explosion erupted from his rear end, which surprised him, together with the other animals in the barn.

This in turn woke up the chickens and the ducks, all of them squawking in surprise, and a few laying extra eggs in fright. Some of the other animals that stayed in the barn, just sleepily opened their eyes, turned over and went back to sleep, hardly bothered at all. Janet and Isiah, the two goats didn't seem too worried either. They just looked at each other, raised their eyes heavenwards, as if to say there he goes again, and carried on munching their hay.

Grandma Megan's homestead is tucked away down a long country lane on the other side of a little bridge on the outskirts of Friston Forest.

Rosie had come to stay with her grandma at the beginning of the summer to recuperate after a bad bout of flu. Later it had been decided that Rosie re-located to live permanently with her grandma and start at the village school once the new term began after the holidays. Rosie had been desperately unhappy at the school she had been attending in London.

Grandma Megan heard Rosie's anguished cry and sprang to her feet from where she had been sitting on a stool in front of her dressing table. Knocking the stool over backwards in her haste, she turned and ran as fast as she could through her bedroom door and along the landing towards her grand-daughter's bedroom.

Arriving at the door, she hadn't slowed down enough and as she turned to enter the room she tripped and slid on the rug just inside the bedroom door. With both feet now planted firmly on the rug it carried on sliding across the floor. The only way Grandma Megan could stop herself from falling in a heap was to put both hands out in front of her and grab the window ledge when it was within reach.

'Whatever's the matter Rosie dear, are you alright?' she panted, as she straightened up and turned around to look in her grand-daughter's direction.

Rosie's eyes were enormous, both with the fright she had had, together with the unexpected sight of her gran sliding across the room. She gulped and managed to splutter 'Oh G=Gran, you won't believe it.'

'Calm down dear,' soothed Grandma Megan, trying to keep calm herself, but very worried at how pale and distraught her grand-daughter looked. She was feeling rather wobbly herself now, after skidding across the floor like that.

Gathering herself together, Grandma Megan walked across the room, picked up a wooden high-backed chair, and carried it to where Rosie was sitting. Setting the chair down, a little to one side, but still more or less in front of her granddaughter, Grandma Megan sat down, reached across and took hold of one of Rosie's cold hands in both of her own. She said, 'Now dear, take a deep breath and tell me.'

Rosie looked at her gran with large tears in her green eyes. 'D-Dad's alive, I saw him!'

Grandma Megan gasped, and one of her hands left holding Rosie's and flew to her own open mouth. Strange and unusual things had been happening of late, but not in her wildest dreams had she expected Rosie to come out with that statement. Swallowing and trying to appear cool and calm, she urged Rosie to tell her why she thought this.

'Well, you know father didn't return home from one of his trips abroad.' Grandma Megan nodded her head. 'Everyone said he must have had a bad accident and been killed. But his body was never found,' continued Rosie.

'No dear, it wasn't. I think that is one of the reasons why your mother has always found it so hard to accept that he's gone,' said Grandma Megan.

'Well, I just saw him Grandma, and he's not abroad, or dead, or anything. He's somewhere near here too.'

'What are you talking about Rosie? How did you see him? Is there something you haven't told me?'

'Hmmmm, well yes. You see I wanted to practice a bit first before I told you. I've been meditating in the evenings, to help with healing myself, and to get stronger after that awful flu. It makes me feel peaceful and relaxed, and afterwards I do feel stronger. Shortly after I started, I found I could leave my body where it was, and go off flying. I was a little frightened at first but it's an amazing experience, and now that the little faery Trilby, is staying with us, she always comes with me to make sure I'm safe.'

'Oh my,' muttered Grandma Megan.

'Anyway, we were out flying around tonight, and I spotted this big old building in the distance, and decided to investigate. It doesn't look like it's been lived in for years, and is very overgrown. Trilby didn't want me to go too near, but I suppose my curiosity got the better of me, and before I knew what I was doing, I was looking in the first window I came to. It was very dirty, and I couldn't see much, so I went to the next window. This wasn't quite as dirty, and with the moonlight shining in I could make out a few things. Something caught my eye, a movement I think. I looked across and I could just about see a man tied to a chair and he had tape over his mouth. He turned and looked in my direction just then, and I know he saw me too. It was my father Gran, I know it was.

'Did you see anyone else?' Grandma Megan asked quietly.

'Not that I remember. I think I must have screamed, and then I was back here again.

'You screamed alright. Gave me quite a turn, I felt my hair stand on end,' said Grandma Megan placing a hand on the top of her head and smoothing back her hair.

'Sorry Grandma, but what are we to do?' asked Rosie, still very agitated.

'Well it's far too late to do anything tonight. The best plan, I think, is to go and see the elf elders in the morning. They will know the best course of action.'

'I can't sleep tonight, after this?' Rosie wailed, very agitated.

'You must try dear, otherwise you won't be fit for anything in the morning. Now go and get ready for bed. But Rosie, you must promise me that you won't go out again tonight,' insisted Grandma Megan.

'Ok, I promise,' answered Rosie and looking very downcast walked to the bathroom next to her bedroom to wash and get ready for bed.

Trilby had returned and was sitting on the window sill. She had flown in earlier, but until now she had gone unnoticed.

Suddenly catching sight of her, Grandma Megan addressed the little faery, 'Trilby, did you see what upset Rosie so?'

Trilby nodded her head. Sitting there swinging her legs, she couldn't understand what all the fuss was about.

'Have you been out with Rosie each time she flies?'

'Yes, I can see when she leaves her body, and I follow to make sure she's safe.'

'Thank you, Trilby, that's very reassuring,' replied Grandma Megan.

Trilby shrugged her shoulders, but was inwardly very pleased.

A few minutes later Rosie re-entered her bedroom, climbed into bed, and pulled the covers up to her chin. It was a warm night but she was feeling chilly.

Tucking Rosie in, and placing a kiss on her forehead, Grandma Megan bid Rosie goodnight and quietly left the room. She had a lot to think about and her mind was spinning.

Chapter 2

Grandma Megan is tall and slim and very much older than she looks. Wearing her long dark hair in a bun at the nape of her neck, her skirts are colourful and long, reaching down to her ankles and accompanied by crisp cotton blouses. Her shoes are black slip-ons turned up at the toe. She is a full elf and originates from Oakenveil, the elf village close by which is situated amongst the trees of Friston forest. The elf village is encased in a protective veil which hides it from the inhabitants of nearby villages, elves preferring to be left in peace to live their own lives, and not be pestered by humans.

Cornelius, the great old oak tree, is one of the few ways that the elves come and go from their village. Mostly he is invisible to the outside world but when summoned by the elves, he appears in the glade, if the coast is clear, and opens a small door for the elves to use.

Grandma Megan's daughter, Adele, met James Hepburn, a human botanist in the forest when she was out gathering plants and berries one day, and they eventually married. It is rare that mixed marriages take place but this one was sanctioned and they went to live in London where Adele works as a doctor in a large hospital.

Rosie, their only child and half elf, half human, which made it very difficult for her to settle into the large school in London. The other children sensed she was different but couldn't understand why. Rosie, a very special child has now reached her twelfth year and her powers are manifesting.

The next morning, Grandma Megan, and Rosie, are sitting at the breakfast table together with Avery, a relative of Grandma Megan's who is staying at the homestead, and whom Rosie refers to as Uncle Avery. Avery proudly calls himself an inventor but sometimes things get a little out of control and so the elders in Oakenveil thought it a good idea for him to go and live with Grandma Megan, in case one day one of his inventions went badly wrong and damaged the precious veil that protected their village.

Grandma Megan had conveyed to Avery first thing that morning what had happened the evening before.

Avery turned to Rosie and asked, 'Rosie are you sure? Sometimes in the cold light of day things seem very different.'

'No, no, I'm positive,' she answered earnestly. 'I know what I saw, and I wasn't dreaming.

'Alright then. I don't think we should involve the police now,' he replied. 'Your grandma and I have decided we'll send a message to Oakenveil, and ask the elves for an emergency meeting. I'm sure Wolfric, for one, will be only too pleased to help,' he added smiling.

'But how do we do that?' asked Rosie. 'We haven't the means of summoning Cornelius.'

'No, we don't, not in the same way Wolfric and the others do,' admitted Grandma Megan. 'But, I have my own way, which you haven't seen yet Rosie dear. I hope it still works.

I haven't had to use it for many a year. The elders insisted I have some means of contacting them, when I moved outside of Oakenveil. I wanted it to be easy for your mother and father to be able to contact me if an emergency arose, and so I moved into this cottage.'

Rising from her chair at the kitchen table, Grandma Megan walked across to the large dresser at the other end of the room, and opened one of the bottom drawers. Reaching far into the back, she extracted an ornate mirror, square in shape, about twelve inches tall and five inches across. Carrying the mirror back to the table she sat down and stood it up against the large milk jug.

Rosie was agog, but Avery just smiled his gentle smile and said nothing.

Looking around the table at the two expectant faces watching her, Grandma Megan then reached across to the mirror and gently rubbed the frame in the middle at the bottom. The sound of tinkling bells echoed around the kitchen. 'Fingers crossed this still works,' she whispered.

'We may have to wait a few minutes,' she explained looking at Rosie. But fortunately, they didn't have to wait too long.

'Here we go,' exclaimed Grandma Megan. Rosie and Avery immediately left their seats and stood behind the seated Grandma Megan, all looking expectantly at the mirror. The glass in the mirror clouded over, and then cleared to show Rowena, Wolfric's mother, smiling at them.

'How lovely to see you all, and what a surprise. Is everything alright?' she enquired.

'It's lovely to see you too Rowena, but something has happened, and we need to see the elders as a matter of urgency.'

Rowena knew Grandma Megan wouldn't have used the mirror for anything trivial, and bid her wait while she went and had a word with her husband, Bertrum, one of the elders.

Appearing in the mirror again after only a few minutes, she said, 'Bertrum will be at Cornelius at eleven o'clock to meet you, all being well in the forest. They all knew that Cornelius would not appear and open the door to Oakenveil, if there were humans about.

Chapter 3

They all arrived, albeit a little early at Cornelius, but Bertrum, was already there, patiently waiting for them. Cornelius, ever vigilant was keeping a sharp lookout for intruders, but luckily all was clear.

With swift greetings to Bertrum, he then quickly ushered them all through the small door in the tree. Once they were safely inside, the door swiftly and silently closed, before Cornelius disappeared, leaving only the grassy glade and gently flowing stream to be seen on the outside.

Rosie had been this way before, not too long ago, but it was as if she was seeing it all for the first time, and was again in awe.

Grandma Megan, and Avery, had lived in this village many years before, and so were used to this way of life, and the differences in culture. Rosie on the other hand had only visited recently, and although she had had a quick introduction to Rowena, and the village, she was once again trying to take it all in.

Noticing her grand-daughter was being left behind, Grandma Megan called to her to catch up. Rosie could easily stray down one of the side passages, and she didn't want to lose time by having to search for her, with such an important task at hand.

Grandma Megan addressed Bertrum, and said, 'I'm sorry to have called you away from your duties in the village, but this is urgent and needs careful handling. If you don't mind we'll wait until we're all gathered before I explain.'

'Quite right Megan,' replied Bertrum, leading the way through the tunnel.

Arriving at Bertrum's home, a beautiful tall ash tree with living quarters inside, three stories high, and a large attic above, Rowena was waiting to greet them at the door.

'Megan, how lovely to see you in person again. It seems a lifetime ago that you went to live outside the village, and Avery too, how wonderful. Now where's Rosie? Aaahhh, there you are child. Come on in all of you and I'll get refreshments.'

Grandma Megan, Avery, and Bertrum, went to sit at the large oak table in the middle of the room. There would be other elders joining them shortly.

Rosie went across to Cozy, the armchair that she had sat in when she had visited before. It was such a lovely armchair, large, squidgy and gave wonderful comforting cuddles.

Rowena came back into the room carrying a tray of glasses with a decanter of elderberry wine together with a plate of delicious looking freshly baked golden biscuits.

Just then, there was a knock on the door, and three other elves entered, Fitz, Vartan and Merith.

After quick greetings, they all sat down and Bertrum, looking around the table at each of them said, 'Now that we are all here, I'll leave it to Grandma Megan to explain why she found it necessary to call this emergency meeting. It's got to be serious otherwise she wouldn't have done so, and I must admit I am very curious.'

Rosie, snuggled down in the armchair. She'd every intention of staying awake and listening to the plans that were to be made to rescue her father, but because she hadn't managed to get much sleep the night before, and now felt so safe and snug wrapped up in Cozy, it was just too much. Her eyelids drooped, and before long she was fast asleep.

Recalling all that had happened the night before, Grandma Megan, stopped to take a drink and glanced over to see if Rosie was alright. She was relieved to see her grand-daughter relaxed and asleep. Poor Rosie, she thought, she had looked so tired and pale earlier, but now she had some colour back in her cheeks, and it would do her good to catch up on her sleep.

'Now I'm not calling Rosie a liar,' said Fitz. 'Are you sure it wasn't just a young girl's fancy. She has missed her father very much.'

'Oh yes, I'm sure,' replied Grandma Megan. 'I wouldn't have bothered you otherwise.'

'Hmmm,' mused Fitz. 'Alright then, the first thing to do, is to check out this building Rosie went to. I think I know the one, although we don't use it at all now. Too far out of the way for anything useful you understand, and outside the village. We'll have to wait until dusk. A few of us will go there tonight, and scout around. Then we'll decide the best course of action.'

The others nodded their heads in approval.

'Can't we just go over there and get him now?' enquired Avery, speaking for the first time. He was an elf of very few words, unless he thought it important enough to open his mouth.

'I think it would be best if we check things out first,' answered Bertrum. 'He must have somebody watching him, and maybe others taking it in turns to make sure he is alright. They have obviously kidnapped him for a reason, and after all this time, they wouldn't want anything to happen to him I shouldn't imagine.'

'They sat talking for another hour or so, deciding on the route to use and what to take with them.

'Well I feel a little better now that things are in hand,' said Grandma Megan. She gave a huge sigh before getting up from the table.

'We'll send you a message, and let you know what's happening,' confirmed Bertrum.

'Thank you,' replied Grandma Megan smiling. 'I know Rosie will be anxious. She wanted to head off this morning and bring him back.'

'I bet she did. Brave young girl that.'

The door opened unexpectedly, and Wolfric, Bertrum and Rowena's son, walked in. Only a couple of years older than Rosie in human years, but in elf years he is much older and wiser.

'Oh, I'm sorry,' he said stopping in his tracks. He hadn't expected to see any visitors, and especially not Grandma Megan and Avery. 'What's going on?' he enquired.

Looking across the room he spotted Rosie curled up in the armchair. She was still fast asleep, but not so peaceful now. Her fingers and eyelids are twitching, and low mutterings emitted from her mouth.

'Is she alright?' asked Wolfric, looking at Grandma Megan. Wolfric had grown very fond of Rosie, Grandma Megan, and Avery since they had helped him so much in recent weeks, after he had got himself into a bit of trouble.

'Yes, she's fine, just tired out and worried,' replied his father. He then went on to explain what was going on.

'Anything I can do to help, just say the word,' enthused Wolfric. He was sorry they were all so desperately worried, but at the same time he could sense an adventure looming, and he loved an adventure.

'We'll let you know son,' his father replied smiling, having a good idea what the boy was thinking.

'Well, I think we'll be heading back now. Thank you all so much. It's wonderful knowing you're here,' said Grandma Megan. She turned, smiled and shook each one by the hand. 'Although I love my cottage at the edge of the forest, I do miss this village sometimes,' she admitted.

Avery got to his feet and nodded in agreement.

'Now where's Rosie? She was in that chair the last time I looked,' said Grandma Megan.

'Oh, she's still there,' chuckled Rowena. 'Cozy, is looking after Rosie beautifully.'

They both crossed the room to wake Rosie, and saw all that was visible was the young girl's head. The rest of her was engulfed by the arms of the chair.

'Thank you Cozy dear, you can let her go now.' Cozy reluctantly released her arms, and settled them back in their usual position. The movement woke Rosie, and she sat up with a jolt, forgetting where she was.

'It's alright dear,' soothed her grandma. 'Up you get, we're going now.'

Rosie rubbed her eyes, and tried to clamber out of the chair.

Wolfric stepped forward and said 'Maybe Rosie would like to stay a while. I can show her some more of the village. She only saw a little when she was here last time.'

Bertrum looked across at Vartan, Fitz, and Merith, who all smiled and gave a nod of consent. He then looked at Grandma Megan, and Avery, who both nodded in unison. They all thought the same thing, that it would keep Rosie occupied, and hopefully ease her worry a little.

'How about it Rosie?' Wolfric asked, thrilled that permission had been given.

'Terrific, if I can only get out of this chair,' she replied, struggling to get up.

Rowena leaned forward, stretched out both hands, clasped Rosie's and pulled. They all heard a little groan from Cozy, as if she were loathed to let go, and then Rosie was on her feet.

'We'll be getting back to the cottage now Rosie dear, and I'll expect to see you back there in time for tea. Alright?' asked Grandma Megan.

Rosie nodded, then realizing nothing was about to take place she blurted out 'But what about my father? Aren't we going to go and fetch him?' she asked, dismayed they weren't all going straight away to storm the old building, and perform a heroic rescue.

'That's in hand dear. The elders are going later tonight. We can't all go in daylight, too much of a giveaway,' explained Grandma Megan.

'But….'

'Now, no buts Rosie. It will all work out, you'll see.'

Rosie wasn't at all happy with this, but she could see the sense in their plan. Then quietly saying goodbye to Grandma Megan, Avery, and the rest of the elves, she crossed to the door where Wolfric was waiting for her.

Chapter 4

Walking slowly down the lane beside Wolfric, Rosie could feel the impatient butterflies fluttering in her stomach. It seemed an awfully long time to wait, even if it was only until this evening.

Glancing across at Rosie, Wolfric could see how worried she felt, and wished there was something he could do to help relax his new friend. Suddenly he had an idea.

After walking for a little while, Rosie asked 'Where are we going?' She was feeling anxious and tired, and had started tripping on nothing. She tended to do this when weary or not concentrating properly. Without a full night's sleep and worrying about her father, she wasn't feeling too well either, and found it difficult to show much interest in anything.

They were nearing the edge of the main square now.

Wolfric glanced at Rosie again, and hoped his plan would ease her pain, even if it was for the time being.

'Can we get to the place where I saw my father?' Rosie asked, suddenly feeling hopeful.

'It's too far, from the description you gave the others,' he replied. 'Also, it's on the other side of our realm. But, how would you like to meet a good friend of mine?'

'Ok,' replied Rosie glumly, her hopes dashed again.

'This way,' urged Wolfric, leading the way across a large expanse of open pasture, through a gate on the other side, and over a small wooden bridge that forded the stream.

'Is it much further?' asked Rosie wishing she could sit down.

'Nearly there. Come and sit on this bank over here,' he indicated, smiling at Rosie who now looked quite pale.

Rosie was grateful, stumbled forward, and sat down with a bump, where Wolfric had indicated. Perched on the bank she looked around, and wondered who lived here. She couldn't see any dwellings or signs of life, just the forest not too far away.

Wolfric stood to one side, and reaching down into his right boot pulled out what look to Rosie like a twig from an old tree.

'What's that?' she asked.

'When it's finished, it'll look like it should do. A flute. It's a project I must do for one of my exams at school. I haven't finished the outside yet, because I want to get to know it first, and make sure it plays the sounds I need.'

Putting one end of this into his mouth, Wolfric blew into it softly. He moved his fingers swiftly covering and uncovering the small holes down the length of the wood.

Rosie had never heard anything so beautiful. Feeling very peaceful now, sitting in the warm sunshine, she closed her eyes, and listened intently to the music.

With the last notes fading away, Wolfric lowered the instrument, and sat quietly.

'Don't fall asleep Rosie,' he said quietly. 'I can hear Oonie approaching. Just sit still, no sudden movements. He's quite shy until he gets to know you.'

Rosie opened her eyes and looked at him. What a funny thing to say she thought. Was this person a hermit or something?

A movement at the edge of the forest caught Rosie's eye. Turning her head to look, she couldn't see anything much at first, just a kind of bright shimmering mist. That's funny, she thought to herself, why would there be a mist on a beautiful day like today. Then she couldn't help a quick intake of breath, and her jaw dropped.

Appearing out of the mist and standing there motionless, but looking straight at Rosie was the most magical being she had ever seen.

Wolfric chuckled quietly. He just loved surprising this young gentle girl. 'You're gaping Rosie,' he whispered.

She snapped her mouth shut then asked, 'Wolfric, why didn't you tell me?'

'It wouldn't have been a surprise then would it. Just sit still. He'll probably come over and inspect you. Don't touch him just yet.'

Sitting riveted to the spot, Rosie sat and gazed in awe. Walking slowly and gracefully towards them, was a unicorn, so white and pure he dazzled her eyes. His horn was bright silver as were his hooves. Oonie knew Wolfric very well, and welcomed seeing him, but he wanted to check out this other visitor.

There was enough room between Rosie, and Wolfric, for him to circle Rosie, and stopped when he was once again standing in front of her.

'Hello Rosie, my name is Oonie.'

'You can talk,' spluttered Rosie. 'And you know my name, has Wolfric mentioned me?'

'Of course, I can talk, but I only do so to those I want to understand me, and no, Wolfric hasn't spoken to me about you, but I have been waiting for you to arrive for quite a while now, as have a lot of others.'

'Why?'

'I expect everything will be explained to you shortly. It is not my place to be the one to do so.'

'Are there any more of your kind?' Rosie enquired, intrigued.

'Oh yes.'

'In the forest, here?'

'In this forest, and some others. Tell me Rosie, can you whistle?'

'What a funny thing to ask,' she replied, and couldn't suppress a giggle.

'Not really. If ever you need help in the future, you have only to whistle, and I will be
there. I will hear you. In this realm or out of it.'

Rosie sat for a moment or two feeling a bit silly. Then inhaling deeply, she puckered up her lips and blew as hard as she could.

Wolfric burst out laughing. Rosie had blown the juiciest raspberry he had ever heard.

Oonie, quickly glanced across at Wolfric, and gently shook his head in warning. Turning back to Rosie, Oonie instructed, 'Put two fingers just inside your mouth, curl up your tongue and blow, gently to begin with, and then a little harder.'

Rosie did as she was asked, thinking to herself that this wouldn't work. She tried once, twice and was just about to give up when suddenly an ear-piercing whistle echoed all around them.

'Wow, did I do that?'

'You did,' whispered Oonie, who was blinking rapidly.

'I think she's got the hang of it now,' muttered Wolfric, who had an index finger stuck inside one of his ears, and was jiggling it about trying to stop the ringing which the loud whistle had caused. Getting unsteadily to his feet, Wolfric addressed Oonie saying, 'I think Rosie had better be getting home now. Her grand-mother will be expecting her home soon.'

Bowing his head, Oonie agreed. But before turning to leave, he addressed Rosie again. 'It has been a pleasure to meet you Rosie. I am sure everything will become clear to you in the not too distant future, and keep practising the whistle, but a little softer, unless you really need to call me.'

'I will,' agreed Rosie. 'Thank you, and it's been so special meeting you.'

Oonie turned and left them, trotting very lightly on his silver hooves back towards the part of the forest he had emerged from shortly before.

'Are you ready to return home now?' asked Wolfric.

'Yes, I'm ready,' she agreed, smiling at Wolfric. 'I feel quite refreshed now, not so tired and depressed.'

'That's good. We'll call in at my home on the way back. I'm sure mother will want to say goodbye to you.'

Chapter 5

Rosie was feeling much happier walking back through the forest after leaving Cornelius. She was humming to herself, and clutching the precious parcel Rowena had given her to deliver to Grandma Megan. Not knowing what was in the parcel, she guessed it must be very important, because Rowena had told her to guard it with her life.

Suddenly Rosie felt something hard hit the back of her head.

'Hey, you there, where do you think you're off to?' called a sneering voice.

'Ouch,' cried Rosie, raising her right hand to rub her head, and at the same time spinning around to see who had done such a thing.

'Who's there? What do you want?' Rosie shouted, trying to keep her voice from shaking.

Out from behind a large holly bush nearby, stepped Jack, closely followed by his mate Charlie. Rosie recognised the two gypsy boys who lived in the camp nearby. A few weeks before, she had helped Wolfric find the golden acorn. He had lost it in the forest one morning whilst collecting plants and berries to take back to his village. Jack, had found the golden acorn, the key used to open the little door of the great old oak Cornelius. Quite an adventure had followed trying to retrieve it, before Wolfric could return home again.

'We were just wondering what you had in the parcel,' said Jack, a greedy look on his face.

Rosie clutched the package tight with both hands, and held it against her chest. Taking a step or two backwards, she managed to reply, 'It's just a gift for my grandma. I'm sure it wouldn't interest you.'

'I think we'll be the judge of that. Hand, it over,' demanded Jack, menacingly, holding out his right hand.

'No!'

'Oooh, brave little thing, aren't you,' jeered Jack.

Both Jack, and Charlie, started moving slowly towards Rosie. She was in two minds what to do. Should she try and brave it out, or take to her heels and run for it. She didn't think she would get very far with, both chasing her.

Before she had decided which action to take, a very bright light shone into both the boys' eyes.

'Aaahhh, put that light out,' they screeched in unison.

'Run Rosie, as fast as you can,' a small voice whispered in her ear.

With a quick intake of breath, Rosie didn't need telling twice and turned and fled through the forest, as fast as her legs would carry her. She had recognised that voice. It was Trilby. What a wonderful little faery, still looking after her. She had thought, Trilby would still be back at her grandma's cottage.

Trilby didn't like accompanying them back to Oakenveil. She was frightened she would never be allowed out again, after the trouble she had caused there in the past. But, she had come into the forest to wait for Rosie, when she saw Rosie hadn't returned with Grandma Megan, and Avery.

Rosie was very thankful Trilby had come looking for her. It proved she was keeping to the bargain she had made, when Grandma Megan said she could stay with them on the condition she behaved herself, and helped Rosie in any way she could.

Trilby kept the light shining in both boys' eyes until she was sure Rosie was almost home. Then with a flick of her hand she upended both boys so their legs flew out in front of them and they landed heavily onto the ground. Satisfied with her handiwork, she flew off to catch up with Rosie, knowing that it would take a few minutes before Jack and Charlie's eyesight returned to normal.

Rosie was almost at the cottage gate. Just a couple of hundred yards or so, and she would be there. She just hoped her legs would hold out. The fright the boys had given her had made them rather wobbly even before she had started running.

Trilby caught up with her at that point, and urged her on. 'Nearly there Rosie, you can do it.'

Gritting her teeth, Rosie stumbled on, still managing to keep a tight hold of the parcel, although it was feeling heavier now.

She was almost there. She could see the gate just in front of her, and she lunged forward and hung over it, her sides heaving and her legs like jelly. Bella, must have heard her because she shot out of the cottage door, barking her head off, closely followed by Grandma Megan.

'What on earth's going on?' Grandma Megan demanded.

Seeing Rosie hanging over the gate she ran to help her grand-daughter.

'Oh Rosie, whatever has happened?' she asked, as she opened the gate enough to squeeze herself through. Putting an arm around Rosie's waist she helped her to stand up. Seeing that Rosie was finding it difficult to catch her breath, she opened the gate wider so they could both get through, and then supported Rosie up the path and into the cottage.

Arriving in the kitchen, Grandma Megan guided Rosie to the rocking chair, which was heaped with multi-coloured cushions, and allowed Rosie to sink down onto the chair. She still hadn't recovered her breath enough to say anything yet, so it was Trilby who explained to Grandma Megan what had happened.

Sitting in the chair still trying to catch her breath, all Rosie could do was nod her head now and again, as she listened to Trilby explaining. She realised she was still clutching the small parcel, and held it out to Grandma |Megan.

'Thank you dear, I completely forgot it. Rowena mentioned she had it, and I was to bring it back with me to the cottage.'

'You …. know what… it is?' Rosie managed to ask, surprised.

'Oh, yes dear, I know. Now, I think you ought to have something to eat and drink. You almost have your breath back, and didn't eat much breakfast.'

Rosie was sure her grandma had changed the subject quickly, before she could ask any more questions, but decided to let the matter drop for the time being.

'I would love a drink of something cool please, my mouth's really dry.'

'I'm not surprised, after all that running,' Grandma Megan chuckled. 'Trilby, would you like something too?'

'I would.'

Grandma Megan stood looking at Trilby, and raised an eyebrow.

'Yes, please, that would be lovely,' said Trilby, and gave a wicked grin.

'Better,' replied Grandma Megan. It was sometimes hard work teaching this little faery some manners, but she was getting there. She went off to fetch Rosie a tall glass of homemade lemonade, and a thimble full of rosehip syrup for Trilby.

Rosie was chattering away to Trilby, when Grandma Megan, came back to the table with the drinks and looking at Rosie, said, 'Well, I'm glad to see you're looking a lot happier than early this morning. Did you have a good time in Oakenveil?'

'Yes, I did, thank you. Wolfric took me to meet a friend of his. His name is Oonie, and he lives in the forest. Have you met Oonie Grandma?'

'Can't say I have dear. The name doesn't ring a bell.'

'We had a lovely conversation, and he was trying to teach me how to whistle,' Rosie explained, proudly.

'Really!' exclaimed Grandma Megan surprised. 'Whatever for?'

'In case I need his help in the future. He has the most glorious white coat that shimmers in the sun, and his eyes are deep blue.'

'Why on earth would he be wearing a white coat in this weather?' asked Grandma Megan, puzzled. 'Does he feel the cold or something?'

Rosie, giggled as she suddenly realised that she hadn't explained properly, then said, 'Oh I'm sorry Grandma, I should have said before, Oonie is a unicorn, and a very handsome one he is too.'

Grandma Megan's hand flew to her mouth. 'Oh my, and to think I've reached the age I am today, and I've never seen one. You're a very lucky girl, Rosie.'

'Yes, I know. He said something very strange though. He said I was special, and he'd been waiting for me for a very long time. What did he mean Grandma? I also heard Rowena say that to Wolfric a little while ago, that I was special, and to look after me. I don't understand.'

Grandma Megan sighed, looked at her grand-daughter and said, 'I was hoping that you'd be able to enjoy your summer and recuperate a bit more, before hearing all this, but I see it isn't going to happen.'

Just then the back door crashed open, and Avery, dashed in, 'Q-Quick Megan, I need help. C-Chicken rugby,' he spluttered. He was out of breath from running around after the chickens, especially when they had started ploughing through Grandma Megan's precious herbs.

'Where on earth did they find one this time,' exclaimed Grandma Megan. 'Sorry Rosie I'll explain everything to you later,' she called over her shoulder as she rushed out of the kitchen door.

Trilby looked at Rosie, and asked 'Chicken rugby?'

Rosie chuckled and said, 'Come and have a look. I bet you've never seen anything like this before.'

Outside the chickens were having a wonderful time. Feathers were flying in all directions. They enjoyed nothing more when they got a little bored, than a game of chicken rugby, using a cherry tomato for the ball.

The game was in full swing when Grandma Megan arrived. She stood for a few seconds watching and deciding the best course of action. She really did enjoy watching them but not when it meant they were going to destroy her well nurtured herbs and plants.

One of the chickens had the cherry tomato in her mouth, and instead of running off to a quiet part of the garden to enjoy eating it, she threw back her head and gave an almighty squawk. This of course alerted the others, who all ran towards her. She then ran off as fast as she could, but when the others caught up with her, they launched themselves on top of her trying to relieve her of the cherry tomato. There was quite a scrum, feathers flying, legs sticking out in all directions, until the chicken underneath opened her beak and the cherry tomato fell out. Another chicken picked it up ran a short distance then threw back her head, gave a triumphant squawk, and the whole thing started again. It lasted until the tomato ended up in bits and was eaten by one and all. There were no holds barred in this game, and Grandma Megan's carefully tended garden ended up looking the worse for wear.

There's only one thing for it, thought Grandma Megan, and she quickly went to fetch a bucket of water, and threw it over as many of the chickens as she could.

'That should cool them off for a little while,' she muttered, putting the bucket down on the ground and wiping her hands on her apron. The chickens didn't mind this at all and every one of them turned their attention to grooming themselves, and tending to the feathers they had left.

**

Back in the forest Jack, and Charlie, were now getting gingerly to their feet, looking about them warily, and rubbing their backsides which were feeling rather bruised after landing so heavily.

'I don't know about you Charlie, but I used to enjoy coming into the woods,' Jack whispered. 'Weird things keep happening now.'

'I know how you feel mate,' replied Charlie. 'I'm getting quite jumpy, and me ma keeps giving me funny looks, when I spook at nothing.

'Come on, let's head back to the camp before anything else happens,' suggested Jack. 'I could do with a drink anyway.'

Charlie agreed and they both started walking, each one limping a little and feeling sore from thumping down on the hard ground.

Chapter 6

Trilby, the mischievous faery, was out in Grandma Megan's back garden the next morning. She wasn't under the spell any longer that had been placed upon her, turning her into a little doll, and so stopping her causing mayhem wherever she went. Now she was thoroughly enjoying her freedom.

Rosie had spotted the little doll sitting on a shelf in the toy shop, the day Wolfric had taken her to see his village, and show her around. Rosie had fallen in love with the little doll on sight, dusty and dirty though she was. Noticing this, Wolfric had presented Rosie with the doll as a thank you gift for helping him in the past.

The spell had broken once the little doll had left the elf village, and that same night there had been a full moon. She changed back to being a forest faery. Rosie had given her the name Trilby, and permission from the elf elders was given for Trilby to stay with Grandma Megan all the time she behaved herself. Grandma Megan stipulated also, that if she misbehaved at all, she would be sent straight back to the village, and put back onto the shelf in the toy shop for all her days to come. She also had to promise to help Rosie in any way she could. Being a mischievous faery, Trilby was finding it more than a little difficult to be good, but she was trying her best.

Flitting about the garden, busy dead heading the flowers that needed attending to, Trilby also made sure that Grandma Megan's herbs were fresh and had enough moisture to keep them growing strong. There was a large variety of herbs which Grandma Megan used for cooking and for medicinal purposes. Her kitchen, full of jars and packets, also had some bunches of herbs hanging up to dry for use later in the year.

Finishing the main garden to her satisfaction, Trilby found herself looking at Rosie's small patch and happily noticed everything was flourishing. Rosie and Grandma Megan had planted everything here only a short time ago, and Trilby was making it her business to take good care of it.

Standing on a small boulder Trilby's eyes alight on the little gnome.

'He's always asleep,' she muttered. 'How can he sleep so much?'

Just then Grandma Megan happened to walk across to Trilby, and heard her. 'He's a garden gnome Trilby dear. They aren't supposed to do anything. They're ornaments, and add interest to gardens.'

'Oh,' replied Trilby thinking this was a daft idea.

Grandma Megan, satisfied Trilby was behaving herself, smiled, and continued to check all the animals she shared the homestead with, making sure they were safe and well.

Watching her go, Trilby decided that something needed to be done with this so-called garden ornament. If she had to earn her keep then so could he.

Jumping down from the boulder, she made her way to the front of the gnome. Standing with her legs apart and a hand on each hip, Trilby opened her mouth and as loud as she could, shouted, 'Wakey, wakey, rise and shine.'

Nothing happened, not even a twitch. 'How rude,' Trilby grumbled. 'Drastic measures are needed here I think,' and before you could blink an eye, Trilby produced her wand. There was a loud crack, together with a green puff of smoke, as she bashed the little gnome smartly over his head with her wand, whilst saying a few words in fae language.

The eyes of the little gnome flew open. Sky blue in colour they look very startled.

'There you are!' exclaimed Trilby beaming at him, very pleased with herself.

The little gnome blinked quickly a couple of times, but didn't utter a sound.

'Cat got your tongue?' asked Trilby, her face so close to his that their noses nearly touched.

'Maybe you can't talk either,' Trilby mused aloud, and gave him another crack on his head.

'Ouch, do you have to do that so hard?' grumbled the little gnome screwing up his face.

'Ha!' gloated Trilby. 'Well, now you can see and talk, I'm going to have to do it again
so, then you can move,' and before he could ask her to just
wriggle her wand, she had cracked
him over the head yet again.

'Yeow.'

'You're welcome,' replied Trilby, pleased with her handiwork. 'Now, try moving your
arms,' she instructed.

'I can't,' he moaned. 'They seem to be stuck. I'm not supposed to be able to do this you know.'

'Right, well start by wriggling your fingers. I had to go through something like this recently, and I know it will hurt, but no pain, no gain as they say.'

'Who's they?'

'Never mind, just try.'

Concentrating very hard, the little gnome managed to move a couple of fingers on his right hand and his thumb on the left.

'Oh dear,' exclaimed Trilby. 'I can see this is going to take a while. You must keep trying. You have to do something to help yourself, you know.'

'Why? Why couldn't you just leave me in peace?' he groaned.

'Well for one thing, I don't think it's right that you just stand around doing nothing day and night. And for another I may need some extra help in the not too distant future.'

'What do you mean?'

'I will explain later, but for now you have got to get yourself moving,' urged Trilby.

'I'm trying, but it's just not easy.'

'I know, I know.' Trilby was starting to feel sorry for the little gnome when she noticed the tears of pain and effort fill his eyes and trickle down his cheeks.

'I can't watch this any longer,' she groaned, and quick as a flash bashed him over the head again.

The little gnome's arms shot up into the air and he yelled again. '*Yeow!*'

'That helped, didn't it? At least your arms are moving. Now try your legs.'

Glancing at Trilby, and feeling very nervous, he was determined to do this as quickly as he could. He didn't think his head could stand another crack. Sliding his left foot forward an inch, he then followed it with the right one, and stood wobbling a little.

'You'll soon get used to it,' said Trilby happily.

'If you say so, but now please explain why you couldn't just leave me alone.'

'Rosie, the girl who rescued you from the garden centre, is going to need help, and I thought the more the merrier, and decided to pick you,' said Trilby.

'But what can I do?'

'I don't know yet. But you must be able to do something, other than stand around day and night surely.'

'I really don't know, I've never tried,' he answered.

'Well you aren't a statue anymore, so try something.'

The little gnome closed his eyes, held his breath, and screwed up his face.

'What are you doing?' asked Trilby, laughing.

'Trying to do magic,' he replied, starting to breathe again.

'Ooohhh.' Trilby lifted her right arm and launched a bright white light at him.

Expecting another crack over his head the little gnome hunched his shoulders and closed his eyes tight.

After several seconds with no assault on his head, he thought it safe to open just one eye to see what was going on. He was amazed at what he saw and opened the other eye to make sure he wasn't imagining it. Some sort of dust was falling all around him and settling on his clothes and skin.

'What's happening, and what is this stuff?' he asked, in a shaky voice.

'Faery dust,' replied Trilby, softly.

'What?'

'Magical faery dust,' said Trilby. 'Now you must be very careful, because I've given you certain powers which you will need, if you're going to help me to help Rosie.'

'What sort of powers?' asked the little gnome, wanting to brush the dust off himself, but not daring to.

'I will explain more later, but for now, you have to get used to walking, running, talking etcetera, etcetera.'

Grandma Megan was standing in the doorway of the barn watching, and wondering, what on earth Trilby was up to now. She had just finished checking Hector the pony, and the two goats Janet and Isiah, together with Zelda the donkey, and all the ducks, chickens and other wildlife that stayed at the homestead making sure they were all well. Looking across to where she had last seen Trilby she had been in time to see the little faery shower the gnome with faery dust.

Walking across to where Trilby was again standing on the boulder, Grandma Megan didn't look at the little gnome, but addressed the little faery. 'Trilby, please explain what you are doing.'

'Well I'm not being naughty if that's what you think,' Trilby replied haughtily, straightening her back and standing as tall as she could, which wasn't a lot. 'I thought we might need some extra help with the quest to find and rescue Rosie's father. He's just been standing there doing nothing, so I used a little magic and put some life into him,' she explained, pointing at the little gnome.

'Put some life into me,' spluttered the little gnome. 'She bashed me over the head, and gave me quite a shock. She's bent my hat too, it'll never be the same.'

'I think it looks better like that,' said Trilby.

Grandma Megan spun around to look at the little gnome.

'Oh my,' she gasped. 'You're talking.'

'I am, and that faery says I can walk too, after she gave me another bash over the head. Then she threw dust all over me,' he replied.

'Trilby?'

'Well, I thought it was a good idea, and when I gave him his voice, I made sure he spoke English, and elven, and understood everything.'

'Maybe so,' said Grandma Megan. But you should have checked with me first. And I also think you could have been gentle about it.'

Addressing the little gnome Grandma Megan asked, 'What shall we call you then, we can't just call you Mr Gnome. Any ideas?'

He shrugged his shoulders, and looked puzzled.

'Titch,' piped up Trilby.

'Behave yourself Trilby,' admonished Grandma Megan. But Trilby wasn't to be silenced and came back with, 'Short Pants, Wee, Mini, Puny, Teeny-Weeny.'

'Trilby, I won't tell you again. If you can't suggest a sensible name, please keep quiet. I think the best thing is to wait until Rosie comes back from the village. She went to take something to Mrs Bennett for me, and she's very good at choosing fitting names.' Turning and looking about her, she asked, 'What's that weird noise?'

'I think it's me,' confessed the little gnome. 'It seems to be coming from my middle.'

'Good gracious me,' laughed Grandma Megan. 'Your stomach is telling you to eat something. You didn't need to eat when you were an ornament, but you do now. We need to get you to the kitchen for some food and drink.'

'That might take some time,' said Trilby, as the little gnome tried a couple of steps forward, wobbled, and fell over backwards his legs waving at the sky.

'Trilby,' admonished Grandma Megan, as Trilby started laughing.

'Right, if you don't mind Mr Gnome, I'm going to lift you up and carry you,' said Grandma Megan, in a kind voice.

'If you say so,' he replied. And with that Grandma Megan bent down, placed a hand either side of his waist and swung him up to sit on her left hip.

'Ooohhh, much better vantage point,' he said grinning, and Grandma Megan set off walking slowly towards the kitchen, with Trilby flying close to her head making faces at the little gnome.

Avery, having a break from his latest project, was standing leaning against his workshop door with a mug of tea in his hand. He watched Grandma Megan walking towards the kitchen carrying the little gnome, and he could swear she was talking to him. Shaking his head, he turned and went back into his workshop thinking to himself things seem to get stranger and stranger by the day here now.

Chapter 7

Rosie was returning to her grandma's through the flower strewn field at the rear of the cottage, heading for the back gate.

Hector, the pony, out in his paddock, had seen her coming, and given her a lovely whinny in greeting whilst cantering to the fence bordering the field. She waved to him and carried on walking hoping he wasn't going to jump the fence.

Marissa, the little Morris estate car, also gave her one of her special whistles in greeting, which alerted Grandma Megan that Rosie had returned.

'That's Rosie back, and is she going to get a surprise,' grinned Grandma Megan, looking at the little gnome and then Trilby.

The kitchen door opened and Rosie walked in. She was about to start telling her grandma about her visit to Mrs Bennett, when she caught sight of the little gnome sitting at the table.

A chair had been piled high with cushions for him to sit on, making it easier for him to reach his plate and cup.

'Moby Dickens,' spluttered Rosie who always said this because she wasn't allowed to swear when surprised or frightened. 'How did that happen?

'Trilby,' replied Grandma Megan. 'She thought we might need some extra help and used her magic.'

'Well that was a nice thought,' acknowledged Rosie grinning at Trilby. 'But what does the little gnome think about it?'

'He'll get used to it,' retorted Trilby before Grandma Megan, or the little gnome, could reply.

'Well, we can't keep calling him the little gnome, so I thought it would be better to wait for you to return and choose a name for him Rosie. Trilby has come up with some very inappropriate ones,' Grandma Megan informed her granddaughter.

Trilby though it advisable to sit still and say nothing, although she did sigh deeply.

'Rosie studied the little gnome, and it only took a minute or two before she came up with the name Cyan, which is a blue-green colour.

'Where on earth did that come from,' asked Grandma Megan surprised. 'I've never heard of that.'

'It's the colour of his hat,' explained Rosie. 'It's one of the colours in my paint box and matches it exactly.'

Grandma Megan nodded and turning to the little gnome asked,' Well, what do you think of the name Cyan, for yourself?'

He tried whispering it a few times, then louder and said, 'Yes, Cyan, I like it very much.

'Good, that's settled then, Cyan it is.'

'Like my names better,' Trilby said quietly. Cyan is too posh for him.'

Grandma Megan turned and gave Trilby one of her stern looks before heading off to fetch Rosie something to eat and drink after her outing. Trilby knew she had better take heed and keep quiet.

Rosie sat watching Cyan, who was busily munching away on the goodies Grandma Megan had set out before him. Tasting a little of this and a little of that she could tell from the expressions on his face what he liked and what he wasn't too keen on. Abruptly she sat up straight in her chair realising what she was witnessing, but she wasn't quick enough to stop him. Cyan had reached across the table, picked a small radish from a nearby bowl, popped it into his mouth, crunched down hard and started to chew. His eyes now looked enormous and he was turning very red in the face.

'Oh no,' gasped Rosie. 'Quickly Cyan, spit it out,' urged Rosie, and he did just that. Not neatly into his hand, or into the serviette by his plate, but blew it out of his mouth with such force that it whizzed past Trilby, who was perched on the back of the chair opposite, nearly knocking her off it.

'Charming, there's gratitude for you,' she grumbled, hanging on tightly to the top of the chair.

'Quick Cyan, drink some buttermilk, it will help to cool your mouth,' urged Rosie handing him the glass.

'What's going on?' asked Grandma Megan returning to the table.

'Cyan just tried one of your extra strong radish,' explained Rosie.

'Oh dear, I forgot to remove those from the table. They're to go into a special chutney I'm planning on making for Fred Bennett, and his wife. They enjoy something with a bit of a kick.

'I think they'll do the trick,' agreed Rosie laughing.

Cyan was sitting holding his glass of buttermilk with both hands up to his mouth trying to cover as much of his tongue and mouth with the cool liquid as he possibly could.

'It'll take a little while for the burning sensation to ease I'm afraid Cyan. Those have a very peppery flavour,' explained Grandma Megan.

Cyan did look a bit of a sorry sight. Raising his eyes to look at her, tears spilled down his cheeks which were still very red.

Let me fetch a cold flannel and wipe your face,' she said and bustled off to fetch one.

Returning very quickly she gently eased the glass from his fingers, wiped away the tears and placed the flannel on his forehead. Hold that there for a while, it should help,' she instructed. Cyan had a better idea though, and grabbing the flannel jammed as much of it as he could into his mouth.

'Yes, well, whatever helps,' said Grandma Megan, and sat down at the table.

Rosie took a drink from the glass of fresh orange juice that Grandma Megan had just placed in front of her and said, 'You were going to explain something important to me yesterday, Grandma. What was it?'

'Ah, yes I was, wasn't I, she replied. 'Well it can't be put off any longer now. 'We have all been waiting for you for a very long time, Rosie dear.'

'I don't understand,' said Rosie really confused now.

'You have heard it mentioned on a few occasions lately that you're special.'

'That's right,' confirmed Rosie her eyes never leaving her grandma's face.

'It was foretold by an elf sage, an elf who possesses strong intuitive powers, a long time ago that someone with strong magical powers and a great healer would be coming to take the place of the one who had held that position, but who had died. None of us knew who it would be and never in a million years would I have guessed that it would be a granddaughter of mine.'

'Why me,' squeaked Rosie.

'Because my beautiful grand-daughter, you are half human and half elf. That doesn't happen very often, not often at all. You know a lot about the human world, after living most of your life in London with your mother, and are quickly, now you are here with us, learning about the elf world. This apparently will be needed in the future. None of us are sure why this is so, but it is. You're a very strong healer already Rosie, and your many other talents are manifesting themselves day by day. There is nothing to be frightened of, Rosie love,' Grandma Megan assured her grand-daughter quickly, seeing the fear on Rosie's face.'

'This is all too much to understand,' Rosie whispered staring at Grandma Megan with huge frightened eyes.

'I know dear, but try not to worry, we're all here to help you, and look after you.'

'That's reassuring anyway,' replied Rosie.

'Well look how you helped Wolfric, when he lost the golden acorn a little while back. Who else could he have called upon for help? No human would have taken him seriously, and they would probably have locked him up somewhere through ignorance, and maybe fear, because they aren't too sure we exist, only maybe in fairy stories.

'Oh, I see,' said Rosie feeling a little calmer now. So, it's because I can interact between both worlds.'

'That's right dear. We need help now too as it happens.'

'Why?' Rosie asked, fear fading and curiosity getting the better of her.

'Something vitally important has gone missing. I don't know, we seem to be losing things left, right, and centre these days,' Grandma Megan, mused with a faraway look on her face.'

'Grandma?' prompted Rosie.

'Mmmmmm? Oh, yes dear, yes, now, where was I?'

'Something vitally important has gone missing. What is it?'

'It's the little silver cup. It's in the shape of a beaker really without a handle, and not very big at all. Also. it's small enough to be slipped into a pocket, or hidden on a person, or elf, quite easily,' explained Grandma Megan.

'Why is it so important? Can't the elves make another one? They seem very good at making anything that's required.'

'No dear, this cup is different. It has special magical qualities, although the magical side of it won't do the human society any good, but it's vital for Cornelius. It was made so long ago when the village was first built, and can't be replaced.'

'What would Cornelius want with a cup?'

'It saves his life dear. That little package Rowena asked you to deliver to me yesterday, is the elixir that's poured into the silver cup and given to Cornelius to drink. Every year Cornelius must have the life enhancing liquid, so he doesn't become sick and die. That would be disastrous for the elf village. Although he's invisible most of the time to the outside world, he's still vulnerable to any disease that might be attacking the forest, and airborne diseases. So, he must have the elixir to keep him strong and healthy. Most of Cornelius is protected by the veil that envelops the elf village, but the part of him that's not, and appears in the glade to open the door, is defenceless against such diseases. If Cornelius gets sick then it could affect the whole of him, the great old oak would be no more, and the veil that protects the elf village will shatter. The elixir must be given to him in the silver cup otherwise it will not work. Cornelius will die.'

Grandma Megan paused, and looked at all the faces staring at her. The silence seemed very loud.

Rosie gulped and was the first to speak. 'How will we know if we find the right cup? There must be a few of them around surely.'

'I'm sure there are my dear, but this one has oak leaves engraved all around the top half and an acorn back and front in the centre. That's where you come in Rosie, my love, because of your powers you will be able to spot it quite easily. It will show itself to you when you're near enough to it.'

Rosie sat staring at her grandma realising the enormity of the task before her. 'But what if I fail and can't find it.'

'I have every faith in you Rosie, and you'll have all the help you need when the time comes.'

'But what about my father? We have to rescue him too.'

'But of course, we do, and that's all-in hand. The elders are searching again tonight, and we'll do everything possible to bring your father home safe and sound.'

'So now we have two quests, my father and the silver cup,' said Rosie. Then a thought suddenly struck her, 'No, we'd better make it three, because we have to save Cornelius too.'

'See, I told you we'd need extra help Titch,' piped up Trilby, looking across at the little gnome.

'Cyan,' he reminded her. 'My name is Cyan.'

'Whatever,' replied Trilby shrugging her shoulders.

'Grandma, where has the silver cup disappeared from?' asked Rosie.

'It's always been kept in its own little cabinet, which is kept locked in the meeting room the elders use to discuss important village matters. I don't think the cabinet is opened very often, only when the silver cup is required for Cornelius. The cup was made for that specific purpose. So, it won't be of any use to whomever has taken it, unless of course they want to cause harm to Cornelius or the elf village.'

'Who on earth would take it,' Rosie asked aghast.

'Well it's got to be someone who knows about it, and where it's kept,' answered Grandma Megan. 'The elves all know about it, and how important it is. But they've been advised by the elders to keep the knowledge to themselves. Maybe one of them was talking about it, and overheard by an outsider.'

'Outsider?' asked Rosie.

'Yes dear, other elves and some folk from different villages come to trade on market days. They have a different entrance to get into the village, because of their carts and such, and this entrance is used only on those specific days, and opened from inside Oakenveil, rather than through Cornelius.

'Oh, I see, so it could have gone anywhere,' said Rosie.

That's what I'm afraid of,' admitted Grandma Megan. 'The elves have searched Oakenveil from top to bottom I understand, but if it's gone further afield, then it's going to be much more difficult to find.'

'When was it last seen?' asked Rosie.

'About a week ago, Turin, one of the elders, took it out of the cabinet to clean ready for use.'

'So, it hasn't been gone long then.'

'No, not that long. I should have received the cup first, and then the elixir a few days later. That's what was in the parcel you carried back for me Rosie dear, the elixir. The cup and the elixir are never delivered at the same time for safety's sake. It has fallen to me to make sure Cornelius receives the drink on the next new moon. So, we only have a short time to find the cup I'm afraid, Rosie dear.'

'No pressure then,' whispered Trilby.

Rosie gulped, and said, 'I think I need some fresh air Grandma. I'll just be in the field at the back. I need to think about all this, and get it straight in my head.'

'Good idea Rosie love. I know it's a big responsibility for such a young girl like yourself, but I have every confidence that you'll do your best.'

Rosie got up from her chair, walked to the back door let herself out, and closed it quietly behind her.

Grandma Megan looked at Trilby, and Cyan, who were motionless staring back at her as if they couldn't believe what they had just heard.

'I think I'll make myself a nice strong cup of tea,' she said, and getting up walked across to fill the kettle and put it on the hob to boil.

Trilby suddenly made up her mind and said to Cyan, 'You just stay put and enjoy your munchies. Myself, I'm going to keep an eye on Rosie and make sure she's alright,' and with that she flew up into the air, out of the open window, and off towards the one-hundred-acre field.

Chapter 8

Rosie was slowly walking along the edge of the field not concentrating on where she was going. Her brain was in a turmoil. How was she going to cope with the tasks ahead of her, and where should she start? So many are counting on her.

Voices close by snapped her back out of her daydream. Recognizing them as belonging to Jack, and Charlie, she frantically looked around for somewhere to hide. Just up ahead she saw a gap in the thick hedge and hurriedly ran towards it, dived in, hoping it was big enough to conceal her. It was quite spacious in the middle, with soft moss covering a large mound which she gratefully sank down on trying to make herself as small as possible. She hoped the boys hadn't caught sight of her.

'So, when are we going to start treasure hunting again?' Rosie, heard Charlie ask Jack.

'Are you still up for it then? I don't like to admit it, but we got quite a fright the last time we were in the forest. Those weird noises, and queer goings on,' replied Jack.

'I know,' said Charlie. 'But if we don't keep on investigating we're never going to find anything, are we? And you did find that golden acorn a little while ago, although that vanished mysterious.

'Don't remind me. Spooky that,' said Jack, giving a little shiver. 'Ok, if you're up for it, how about we start again tomorrow?'

'Great,' replied Charlie, grinning at his mate. He still had visions of finding a stash of treasure somewhere in the forest.

Rosie sat very still until she was sure the two gypsy boys had walked far enough into the distance before she decided to move and leave her hiding place. Although she hadn't been hiding very long, she had been sitting with her legs tucked underneath her and now getting to her feet found she had pins and needles in her legs making her unsteady. Stumbling forward she grabbed at the nearest branch. Unfortunately, this was old and brittle, and broke off with a loud crack, sending her toppling to the ground. Rosie landed with a thud and was grateful that the mound was soft underneath her. But her relief was short lived. She felt the ground moving, and before she could do anything to save herself she was falling, down and down. It was as if the earth had opened and swallowed her.

'Aaahhh!' screamed Rosie.

'What was that? Did you hear it?' Jack asked, stopping in his tracks.

Charlie nodded at his mate, and both took to their heels and ran for all they were worth.

After what seemed an age to Rosie, she landed in a heap on the earthen floor. It was very dark, and she felt as if all the breath had been knocked out of her. Slowly, she moved her arms and legs making sure nothing was broken. Relieved she was alright if maybe a bit bruised, she found she had room to move without any difficulty. What had happened? Where was she? What was she to do?

Sitting there she couldn't decide. She felt as if she had fallen quite some distance. Maybe if I try to climb back up, she thought.

'Would you mind moving your left foot,' said a small voice, making her jump.

'Moby Dickens, whose there,' said Rosie, her voice trembling.

'My name is Erin, and your foot is on my tail,' came the reply.

'Your tail? What are you?' asked Rosie, moving her foot a little to the right. She could just make out a shape of some sort, now her eyes had started adjusting to the gloom. She sensed a movement, and then two large golden eyes were peering into hers. Her head shot backwards in surprise when a cold wet nose touched the tip of her nose.

'I am a silver dog fox if you must know, and you have just destroyed my cosy hollow,' Erin accused her. 'I've been up all night, hunting, and had just settled down for a nice rest when you blundered in. I had arranged it how I wanted it too.'

I'm sorry,' apologized Rosie. 'I had to find somewhere to hide so those gypsy boys wouldn't see me,' she explained.

'Oh, I know all about them,' said Erin. They're always setting traps, and we all have to be extra careful when out and about.'

'Mmmmm. Do you have any idea how I can get out of here? I was thinking of maybe climbing back up, but I think it's very steep and quite a long way to the top,' said Rosie.

'No, I haven't a clue I'm afraid. My burrow isn't this side of the forest, and I just use the hollow every now and then,' said Erin.

It suddenly dawned on Rosie, she was sitting underground talking to a fox, and started giggling.

'What's up with you?' asked Erin. 'Not in shock or anything, are you?'

'No, I'm fine,' replied Rosie. I've just realized I'm sitting at the bottom of a great hole, chatting away to a fox. Must be another one of my talents emerging,' she said.

'Well you're the one we've all been waiting for, aren't you?' he asked.

Rosie nodded her head. Had one and all heard about her?

'Thought so, otherwise you wouldn't have understood a word I've been saying.'

Rosie happened to look up above her just then, and noticed a bright light. It seemed to be coming closer.

'What's that?' she whispered.

They both sat watching and waiting.

Before the light was fully down to them a little voice said, 'Well Rosie, you seem to be in another pickle. It's a good thing I decided to come and keep an eye on you, isn't it?'

'Trilby!' exclaimed Rosie, and then exhaled deeply. 'Oh, am I glad to see you. Thank goodness, your wand gives out a good light. It's been very daunting not being able to see where we are, or what's around us.'

'Are you hurt?' asked Trilby, looking down at Rosie.

'No, I'm fine, thank you. This is Erin. I'm afraid I destroyed his hollow when I stumbled and fell through,' said Rosie.

Trilby nodded at Erin, but he just sat and stared at the little faery.

'Have you any idea how we can get out of here?' Rosie asked.

'Haven't a clue,' replied Trilby.' You can't climb back up. Too Steep.'

'Well at least we can see where we're going now,' said Rosie, relieved. Looking about her, she noticed a couple of passageways. One was leading off to the right, and the other went straight ahead. 'Which way do you think we should go?'

'Let's try the passage to the right,' suggested Trilby. 'It looks as if it's been used recently so it must lead somewhere. If not, then we'll come back and try the other.'

'Alright,' agreed Rosie, getting to her feet. 'I wonder how long this tunnel has been here. It's quite big and dry, and at least I can stand up straight in it. I wouldn't have fancied crawling along on my hands and knees.'

The tunnel was well built with wooden uprights and crossbeams strategically placed for safety and to stop the whole thing caving in. It was just unfortunate Rosie had found the one weak spot in the whole of the tunnel.

Trilby lead the way. Rosie followed close behind with Erin at her heels. The wand gave plenty of light so they could all comfortably see where they were going.

'There's been work going on down here recently by the look of it,' said Rosie noticing the holes in the walls, and large chunks of stone here and there.

They had been walking for some and quite a distance, or it felt like it to Rosie. 'I hope we come to the end soon. I'm starting to feel claustrophobic,' she admitted, and tripped over something. Looking down she noticed small steps had been dug out, and they were heading upwards. We'll be out soon, she told herself.

They came to a halt at the top of the steps, and were faced with a heavy wooden door, secured with a rusty bolt and lock. 'Well I can't open that,' said Rosie.

'I can,' said Trilby, and tapped it with her wand. The rusty lock sprang open immediately.

Rosie stepped forward, removed the lock and with a bit of effort slid the bolt back.

Trilby extinguished the light from her wand before the door was opened, and carefully put it out of sight until they knew what they were walking into.

Rosie reached forward, lifted the door latch and pulled the door towards her. It squeaked a little but otherwise opened easily enough.

Turning around she looked at Trilby and Erin, put her finger to her lips and whispered, 'Shush, we'd better be very quiet, just in case someone's around we don't want to meet.'

Once through the door, Rosie closed it as quietly as she could. She was surprised to see that once the door was closed it blended in with the surrounding wall, and unless you knew what you were looking for, you would never know there was a way in here. Turning and taking the lead Rosie lead the way down the small passageway until it opened out into a large main tunnel.

'I think I know where we are,' said Rosie, amazed.

'I do too,' said Trilby, very quietly. 'I think I'd like go back the way we came.'

'Don't worry Trilby. You're with me now so you'll be fine,' said Rosie, trying to sooth the little faerie's worries.

'Why is Trilby so worried?' asked Erin, looking up at Rosie.

'This is the main tunnel to the elf village of Oakenveil. Trilby is a mischievous little faery, or she was once, but now she is trying to turn over a new leaf and behave herself. Years ago, she had caused a lot of trouble in the village and a spell was put on her to turn her into a little doll. She was put on a shelf at the back of the toy shop in Oakenveil, and there she stayed for years and years until Wolfric gave her to me as a gift not so long ago. He hadn't been told that she wasn't just a little doll. It wasn't until later, I found out she was in fact a woodland faery. She has since been given permission by the elders to stay with Grandma Megan, and me, as long as she behaves herself,' explained Rosie.

'Oh, I see, that explains it then,' said Erin, looking at Trilby.

'I think we'd better make our way to Wolfric's home, and let them know what's happened. They need to know there's a large hole above the tunnel, and do something to repair it as soon as possible,' said Rosie.

Trilby lingered behind, and couldn't get the thought of being captured and locked up again out of her mind.

'Keep close to me Trilby, and you'll be fine. Don't go flying off on your own,' said Rosie.

Before long they were out of the tunnel and walking down the lane leading to the tree house, Wolfric's home.

Chapter 9

Wolfric was sitting on a wooden stool outside, sanding down the wooden flute he was making for his school project. He preferred working on this part outside in the sunshine, because it became dusty in the workshop.

Glancing up and along the path leading to Cornelius, he was startled to see Rosie walking towards him. Trotting beside her was a magnificent silver fox, and he could just make out Trilby, peeking out of Rosie's top pocket on her cotton blouse.

Springing up from his stool he ran to meet her.

'Rosie how did you get here?' he asked, grinning at her.

'I'll tell you all about it in a minute. Are your parents at home? I need to speak to them urgently.'

'Yes, they're both here. Come with me and we'll find them. I'm very intrigued,' said Wolfric.'

They had now reached the door to the tree house.

'Come along in and make yourselves comfortable,' he said, and went off to find his parents.

Rowena was the first to come and greet Rosie, closely followed by Bertrum.

'What a pleasant surprise my dear,' smiled Rowena. Is everything alright? Come and sit down.'

Rosie chose an upright chair at the table this time, not daring to get too comfortable in Cozy. Erin stayed close to her and lay down at her feet. Trilby had ducked down in Rosie's pocket, and curled up as small as she could at the bottom of it.

Rosie explained to them how she had come to be hiding in the hedge sitting on the soft mound, and how this had given way and she had fallen through and landed in the tunnel.

'Oh sorry, this is Erin by the way,' apologized Rosie, introducing the silver fox. 'I'm afraid I destroyed his hollow unwittingly.'

'Pleased to meet you Erin,' they all chorused.

'Likewise,' he said, bowing his head.

Trilby stayed where she was wishing with all her might, Rosie wouldn't mention she was also with her.

When Rosie had finished speaking Bertrum said, 'This is very serious and needs to be dealt with right away. Although it hasn't been a very nice experience for you Rosie, it's a good thing it did happen otherwise we might never have known there was a breach in our security, especially if it had been a rabbit falling through instead of you. Now if you will all excuse me, I'll go and let the others know. Then we'll start right away with the repairs.'

Bertrum hurried out the door, all eyes watching him go, worried expressions on their faces.

You're a blessing in more ways than one Rosie, dear. Thank you,' said Rowena squeezing one of Rosie's hands. 'Now before you head back to Grandma Megan's – it is getting rather late and she will be worried – I think we need to clean you up a bit.'

Rosie hadn't realised it, but she did look rather a mess with soil and bits of grass in her hair, and dust smudges on her face and clothes.

'Oh gracious, do I look a sight?' she exclaimed, dismayed.

'Well you can't expect anything else after falling down a large hole, now can you?' laughed Wolfric.

'Now, now,' admonished his mother. 'We'll soon have you clean and tidy again dear. Don't look so worried. Come with me.'

Ten minutes later and Rosie was washed and her clothes brushed clean. Rowena knew Trilby was hiding in Rosie's pocket and whilst she was gently brushing the dust from Rosie's blouse, she quietly whispered, 'Don't worry Trilby, I won't say a word.' And with that Trilby popped her head up, and gave Rowena one of her rare beautiful smiles.

'Thank you,' said Rosie, and she gave Rowena a gentle hug being careful not to squash Trilby.

'Now I think you're ready to go back. Wolfric will see you through Cornelius.'

Walking back into the other room where Wolfric, and Erin, were waiting, Trilby thought it was safe now Bertrum had left, so she was head and shoulders out of Rosie's pocket with her little hands holding the top.

'Hello Trilby,' greeted Wolfric. 'It's nice to see you again. Behaving yourself I hope.'

Trilby, being Trilby, just stuck her tongue out at him and didn't bother answering.

Wolfric burst out laughing. 'Ready?' he asked, looking at Rosie.

'Ready,' she agreed, and they set off along the path. Rowena stood in the doorway watching them go.

Chapter 10

Grandma Megan was busy preparing the evening meal and wondering what was keeping Rosie. She wasn't worried. She knew her grand-daughter would be sorting everything out in her head. Rosie was learning a lot about herself in a short space of time, and Grandma Megan was sure she would take it all in her stride and cope.

Bella was sitting at the open kitchen door waiting patiently for Rosie to return. She had washed and seen to the little kitten Amber earlier and who was now fast asleep in Bella's bed.

Grandma Megan had made a comfortable little bed for Cyan too, in a Moses basket, and he too was fast asleep in the far corner of the room. It had been a very busy and tiring day for him. Little snores emanated from the Moses basket. Grandma Megan looked around the kitchen and smiled. Her family was getting larger by the day and she loved it.

Bella stood up, gave a little bark and ran to the other side of the room.

Strange thought Grandma Megan. If it was Rosie returning, Bella would normally have run to meet her.

Going to the door and looking out she could see why Bella was anxious. The little dog was making sure nothing was going to harm Amber, and was keeping guard.

'It's alright Bella. No harm will come to Amber, or yourself, whilst you're here with me,' soothed Grandma Megan.

Rosie was nearing the garden gate by now, and Grandma Megan stood watching her grand-daughter. She was pleased to see Rosie was looking so much better, not so fragile.

Rosie stopped at the other side of the gate instead of opening it and walking straight in. 'This is Erin Grandma. Is it alright if he comes in?'

'Of course, dear, come along in.'

Rosie had been worried about the chickens and ducks, but Grandma Megan didn't seem bothered at all.

'I've met Erin before,' said Grandma Megan. 'Fred Bennet, brought him to me when he was a cub. He'd been caught in one of the poacher's traps and had a bad foot for a time. But with my potions and lots of care, it healed beautifully and he was set free when he was old enough to look after himself.

'Oh, I see,' said Rosie.

Looking at the silver fox Grandma Megan enquired, 'How are you Erin? My, but you've grown into a handsome chap.' Grandma Megan also had the ability of conversing with the animals. This was why she was so good with them when they were sick or ailing. They could let her know where it hurt.

'I'm fine thank you, Grandma Megan. I always meant to come by and see you, but somehow, until now I've never seemed to manage it.'

'That's alright dear, as long as you're healthy and happy.'

Erin nodded and followed Rosie through the gate, up the path, and into the cottage.

Bella was on her feet standing in front of Amber ready to protect her if necessary.

'It's alright Bella. I know Erin, and he made a promise a long time ago not to harass or touch any of the animals here.'

Bella visibly relaxed, jumped into her basket and curled up with Amber.

'You're a bit late Rosie dear. Is everything alright? Where did you meet Erin?'

Rosie, once seated at the table then relayed everything that had happened since she had left earlier in the day to go for a walk.

Grandma Megan looked concerned. 'So, do they think this hole can be repaired? That's very important for the safety of the village.'

'I think so,' said Rosie. 'Bertrum was getting the elders and other elves together, and they were all going straight away to inspect it, and do what they could to repair it.'

'That's good,' said Grandma Megan, relieved.

Chapter 11

That same morning Jack, and Charlie, were sitting outside Jack's caravan trying to decide what to do for the day, when the decision was made for them.

Mrs Zarik, Jack's mother, came bustling up to them and said, 'Quick lads, make yourselves scarce. Your father's heading this way Jack, and he's in a fair old rage this morning, for some reason or another.'

Arthur Zarik, had been drinking rather heavily of late, because of the pain in his leg which Jack had broken a few weeks earlier in one of the many fights he had with his father.

The two boys didn't need telling twice, and quickly vanished around the back of the caravan, and ran to the top of the field, then into the forest.

'Where is he?' Arthur Zarik, shouted at his wife. 'I want a word with that little whipper snapper.' He was waving one of his crutches around in the air. His face was bright red and there were beads of perspiration running down it.

Mrs. Zarik shrugged her shoulders, and returned to hanging out her washing.

'Get me a drink woman, can't you see I'm in pain,' he shouted at her, and sank down in a nearby deck-chair throwing his crutches on the ground.

Mrs Zarik, went and put the kettle on to boil some water. She wasn't about to give him any more of the drink he was referring to. A strong cup of coffee was what he was going to get, and if he didn't like it he could get up and fetch it himself, which she knew he wouldn't do.

Jack, and Charlie, had stopped running now they had entered Friston forest, and were ambling along one of the side paths. They were on the far side of the forest this morning which made Charlie feel a bit easier. So many weird things had been happening when they were in the other end of the forest. He was still hoping they would find some treasure, but was beginning to lose heart of ever doing so.

Suddenly Jack grabbed Charlie's right arm, and roughly yanked him behind the nearest tree.

Charlie had just opened his mouth to protest loudly at his mate's rough handling, when Jack put an index finger to his lips.

'Ssshhh,' and he pointed up to where another larger pathway crossed theirs.

They both stood silent and watched.

Two figures were hurrying along the path. One was very tall and thin and the other was shorter and stouter. The taller of the two kept looking furtively about and urging the other to hurry up.

They passed by, close to where the boys were hiding behind the tree, and Jack, and Charlie, clearly heard the shorter one grumbling.

'I don't see why we have to move him now. It seemed a safe enough place to me.'

'Because our lookout said he saw someone, or something, moving around last night, and we can't take any chances now,' replied the taller of the two.

The voices grew fainter as they headed off into the distance.

'Crikey, what was that all about,' whispered Charlie, who now realised he'd been holding his breath.

'Don't know,' replied Jack. 'But you can bet they're up to no good. That tall one was very edgy.'

'Is the carnival in town or something?' asked Charlie. 'They were wearing weird clothes, cloaks and pointy hats. And what was in that wheelbarrow the shorter one was pushing?'

'It was a man, and he was tied up, blind-folded with tape across his mouth,' replied Jack. 'Can't be easy pushing that in the woods.'

'Shall we follow them?'

'Might as well,' answered Jack. 'We've nothing else to do, and I don't want to return to the camp site too early.'

So, Jack, and Charlie, followed at a safe distance as quietly as they could. As usual Jack took the lead with Charlie bringing up the rear, both trying not to step on any dried branches which would crack and give them away.

Jack suddenly stopped in his tracks.

'I wish you'd stop doing that,' grumbled Charlie. 'Can't you hold up a hand or something to let me know you're stopping? I'm getting fed up with bumping into you. What's up anyway?'

'They've gone.'

'What do you mean, they've gone? You had them in sight, didn't you?' said Charlie.

'See for yourself if you don't believe me,' said Jack.

Charlie took a step forward, and looked around the side of Jack who was still standing in front of him. 'Well I can't see a building of any sort, and we weren't that far behind them. Were we?'

'No, we were catching them up if anything,' replied Jack. 'The one with the wheelbarrow was getting slower.'

'Let's walk on a bit further,' suggested Charlie. 'Maybe the trees are blocking out something, and we can't see it from here.'

'Ok,' agreed Jack. 'But we'd still better be quiet, just in case.'

Both boys crept forward looking in every direction hoping to spot something that would indicate where the peculiar pair had gone. Nothing.

Jack stood still scratching his head. 'I just don't believe it,' he said. 'They can't just have vanished.'

'They have,' whispered Charlie.

Chapter 12

Early the next morning, Grandma Megan had fed and watered all the animals and let them out into their various paddocks. The chickens and ducks were happily pecking away in the large back garden, and Grandma Megan was back in her kitchen preparing breakfast for Rosie, and herself.

I'm not really looking forward to giving Rosie the news, thought Grandma Megan as she stood at the stove making scrambled eggs for them both. She had heard some upsetting news from Bertrum, via Mira the mirror link, late last night after Rosie had gone to bed.

'Good morning Grandma,' greeted Rosie, brightly from the kitchen doorway.'

'Oooh you made me jump, Rosie, dear. I was miles away,' admitted Grandma Megan. 'Did you sleep well?' she asked.

'Yes, I did thank you. I went straight to sleep as soon as my head hit the pillow,' said Rosie, waving across to Bella.

'That's good. Now sit yourself down and eat your breakfast, dear,' said Grandma Megan, placing a plate of scrambled eggs on toast in front of her grand-daughter, then pouring a glass of orange juice from the jug to accompany it. She wanted to make sure Rosie ate something first before she gave her the news. She knew her appetite would disappear when she told her the latest. 'Avery has had his already. He was up very early and couldn't wait to get back to his latest project, whatever that might be. I must admit though, it's a blessing we're not being subjected to those loud explosions we had a while ago.'

Rosie nodded her agreement and smiled up at her grandma, her mouth being too full to answer.

Grandma Megan carried on, 'I don't know what he's up to, but he's had one and all in the village saving the cardboard middles to toilet rolls, and when he went to collect some yesterday he returned with quite a bag full.'

Cyan was wide awake now too, and Grandma Megan lifted him up onto a chair at the table, again piled high with cushions. He was now sampling cereal, toast, honey, basically everything Grandma Megan was putting out for breakfast. He found there wasn't much he didn't like, and was thoroughly enjoying himself.

Rosie ate her breakfast and drank some fresh orange juice.

Grandma Megan looked at her grand-daughter and said, 'Rosie dear, I've heard from Bertrum, via Mira the mirror. The elders, and Bertrum, had a good search around the area, including the old building you saw, but I'm afraid they didn't find your father.'

'But they must have done,' Rosie answered dismayed. 'I saw him. I know I did. I wasn't imagining it.'

'I believe you love, but he wasn't there last night. Bertrum did say they'd found evidence someone had been there recently. Did your father wear a ring besides his wedding ring?'

'Yes, he did. It was a special one that mother had made for him as a surprise Christmas present,' said Rosie.'

'Describe it for me Rosie love,' asked Grandma Megan.

'It's a gold band with very small oak leaves standing proud all around the outside. Why?'

'Because they found a ring matching that description on the dusty floor, so it's a good indication your father was there. Whoever has him captive, decided to move him soon after you saw him,' Grandma Megan, explained to Rosie, as gently as she could.

'But now we won't have any idea where they've taken him,' exclaimed Rosie dismayed.

'Well, the elders are now sure he must be hidden nearby, and they will all be keeping their eyes and ears open. I'm sure it won't be too long before he's found. I know it's hard, but try not to worry too much Rosie dear,' said Grandma Megan, patting Rosie's hand.

'Easier said than done,' piped up Trilby, who was sitting on a shelf on the kitchen dresser. She was busy eating honey, and getting in a bit of a sticky mess.

Grandma Megan, just turned and gave the little faery one of her stern looks. 'I have an idea,' she said. 'Why don't we have a trip to the county fair in Hellingly. It's a lovely day and Avery can come too. It will do him good to get out of his workshop for a while.'

Rosie nodded her head, only half listening. Her mind was understandably elsewhere.

Chapter 13

Later that morning, Grandma Megan, Rosie and her Uncle Avery were travelling the country lanes sitting in Marissa, and heading off to the county fair. Grandma Megan had packed a picnic lunch for them to eat when they arrived. She was desperately hoping the music, various stalls and rides would take Rosie's mind of her worries, if only for a short while. So much had happened lately and Grandma Megan wanted her grand-daughter to enjoy herself just like any other young girl, eating candy floss, toffee apples, going on the different rides, together with lots of laughter.

They could hear the music clearly before they arrived at the fairground, and Grandma Megan fleetingly wished she had brought ear plugs with her.

After a quick bite to eat and a drink, they set off and walked towards the funfair. Avery was still munching on a potato and mushroom pasty held in one hand and a mug of tea in the other. Grandma Megan would put the empty mug into a plastic bag when he had finished, and drop it into the carpet bag she always carried with her when they went out anywhere.

Strolling around Rosie started to feel better, and she loved the music. She didn't know what to look at first, and Grandma Megan was pleased to see the delighted smile on her grand-daughter's face and her eyes were positively sparkling. It was a good decision of mine to come here today, she thought. The child can't keep worrying herself sick. That wouldn't do her any good at all.

They stood watching the bumper cars, and Rosie thought it looked great fun. Avery glanced down at her, nodded his head, and before Grandma Megan could stop them, they had climbed up the few wooden steps and jumped into a waiting bumper car. 'I've always wanted to have a go on one of these,' Avery whispered into Rosie's ear.

After paying the lad who had jumped onto the back of their car, Avery shouted, 'Hang on tight, here we go,' and they started to move forward. They hadn't moved very far when they were bumped quite hard from behind. Avery turned his head, and saw a cheeky lad grinning at him. Quickly spinning the wheel, he chased after that car, and got his own back with a hefty bump of his own. Because he had gathered speed chasing him, he almost knocked the young lad out of his seat.

'Gotchya,' shouted Avery gleefully, and was quickly off steering towards another unsuspecting driver. He hadn't had so much fun in a long time, but he still made sure Rosie was enjoying herself and wasn't worried.

All too soon the ride ended and they climbed out. Both laughing happily they re-joined Grandma Megan who had been patiently standing nearby watching.

Rosie, and Avery, were looking around for the next ride, and decided on the swinging boats. This one alarmed Rosie a little, because they were swinging very high before Avery stopped pulling hard on the rope, and they gradually slowed to a stop.

Avery was now heading for the cup and saucer ride after they had clambered out of the swinging boat. He beckoned to Rosie, to follow him. This ride was also great fun although this time Grandma Megan was more than a little alarmed at the speed it was going. Surely, they would topple out?

The next ride they had to try was the carousel.

They could have carried on and on, but Grandma Megan suggested they slow down for a while, and they went across to the candy floss stall. Each had a large stick of the sweet pink fluffy candy.

Spotting a nearby sweet stall Grandma Megan made a beeline for it and purchased toffee apples, liquorice laces, some crystallized ginger - which she was very partial to - sticks of rock and boxes of fudge. She would keep the ginger for herself, but the rest she planned to donate to the school fete to be held shortly.

Rosie purchased a huge whirly multi-coloured lolly pop, and a candy necklace for herself. She then decided to get some satellite wafers, more commonly known as flying saucers, for Wolfric.

Avery treated himself to some Rain-Blo bubble gum. He just loved blowing bubbles even when they became too big and popped all over his nose and mouth so he had to peel the gum off. He also purchased some honey filled assorted fruit candies.

'Well that should keep us going for a little while,' chuckled Grandma Megan as all three walked away with their goody bags. 'I don't know about you, but I could do with a sit down and a nice cup of tea. Let's return to Marissa and head in the direction of home. I know of a little café on the way which should be open.'

Busily making sure that she had stowed all her purchases carefully into her carpet bag so that nothing was squashed, Grandma Megan suddenly realised Rosie wasn't by her side.

'Where's Rosie?' she asked, turning to Avery who was busy unwrapping a piece of his bubble gum.

'She was here a minute ago,' he replied, popping the gum into his mouth. 'She can't have gone far. There she is,' he said pointing a finger.

Grandma Megan quickly walked to where Rosie was slowly turning this way and that and scanning all before her.

Grandma Megan thought Rosie was taking it all in, so she could remember it after they had left and said, 'Don't worry Rosie, love. This isn't the last fun fair we'll be attending.'

'No, it's not that Grandma, I just had the strangest feeling I was being watched. All my hair seemed to stand on end, and I suddenly felt really scared.'

Grandma Megan put an arm around Rosie's shoulders and looked all about them. She didn't notice anything out of the ordinary, everyone seemed to be enjoying themselves and she didn't spot anybody lurking or looking suspicious.

'Come on Rosie, dear, let's go and get that cup of tea, shall we?'

'Mmmmm,' acknowledged Rosie, walking along with her grand-mother but still looking about her.

'Is everything alright?' asked Avery, when they reached where he was standing waiting for them.

'Yes, everything's fine. Shall we go?' suggested Grandma Megan.

Avery continued looking at Grandma Megan, until she silently mouthed, 'Tell you later.'

Chapter 14

Driving along the country lanes they were all very happy. Rosie was feeling safe again sitting in Marissa with her grandma and her Uncle Avery. She was in fits of laughter remembering Avery's face when he kept slipping sideways whilst riding the carousel. 'Your face was a picture,' spluttered Rosie.

'I'm sure that one was polished more than the others, hoping some poor soul would slip off,' he grumbled. 'My legs really ache from gripping the sides of that horse, and I'm sure some of those rides were going faster than they should.'

Avery had been chewing away at his bubble gum and then blew a huge bubble which, of course, burst and splattered all over his face. Rosie, exploded with laughter until her sides ached.

'Ah, here we are,' said Grandma Megan.

The lane had widened considerably, and a couple of hundred yards ahead they turned left into a small carpark. After parking the car, they spotted a sign indicating the way to the café, and headed in that direction.

There was something here for all of them to have a look at after their refreshments. Grandma Megan headed off to the small nursery. She had decided to stock up on some fresh herbs to plant, replacing the ones the chickens had destroyed with their games of chicken rugby.

'You stay close to Avery,' she advised Rosie. 'I won't be long.'

Avery smiled down at Rosie. 'Shall we check out these wooden carvings, and then we can mosey along to the gift shop. After that we'll check out the crystal shop.'

Rosie nodded and happily walked along beside him. The carvings were beautifully done. Quite a little crowd were mooching about and asking the carpenter various questions, such as what type of wood he used, and where he got it from.

Rosie gently tapped Avery's arm. He bent down, and she whispered into his right ear, 'They are very nice, but not as good as yours.'

Avery was thrilled and beamed at her, then whispered back, 'Thank you.'

There wasn't all that much that interested them in the gift shop, so they made their way down the path to the crystal shop.

Looking in the window, Rosie was amazed at all the different colours, shapes and sizes of the crystals displayed.

Entering the shop, she noticed a friendly looking woman sitting at a small table. She smiled at Rosie, and invited her to have a good look around.

'Thank you. I didn't realise there were so many different ones,' admitted Rosie.

'Oh yes, there is something for everyone and everything. Are you looking for anything particular?' asked the woman.

Rosie shook her head and smiled.

'Well you just take your time and have a good look around. Maybe one of them will call to you.'

Rosie stared at the woman. She wondered what the woman meant.

Chuckling at the expression on Rosie's face the woman said, 'You just wait. You'll see what I mean before you leave.'

Rosie nodded her head and walked across to the far wall where the shelves were stacked with necklaces, rings, bracelets, and earrings all with various crystals imbedded in the silver.

She turned to make her way to the next display when she involuntarily took a step backwards. Her head suddenly felt as if it was full of cotton wool, and all her energy seemed to be draining away. It was a good job she had stepped away from the shelves because she suddenly sat down on the floor with a bump. Everything was spinning around her.

Before the shop owner could jump to her feet, the door burst open and Grandma Megan rushed in. She had finished her shopping in the nursery and was looking in the crystal shop window just in time to see what was happening.

Bending over Rosie she whispered, 'It's alright Rosie, love, you'll be just fine in a few minutes. With my help, can you get to your feet? We'll get you outside for some fresh air.'

Helping Rosie up off the shop floor, Grandma Megan put an arm around her grand-daughter's waist supporting her, and they slowly walked out of the shop. The owner was following close behind carrying her chair for Rosie to sit on.

'Thank you,' said Grandma Megan as, she helped Rosie lower herself onto the chair.

'Could we bother you for a glass of water?'

'Of course, I'll be right back,' said the woman and bustled off.

'What's going on?' asked Avery, looking very worried. 'I only went back to the gift shop when I saw you were here.'

'It's alright Avery, don't look so petrified,' Grandma Megan soothed. 'Rosie will be fine shortly.'

'But why? What is it?' he persisted.

'Crystal overload,' Grandma Megan explained. 'Rosie is a very sensitive child. I blame myself. I should have realised, but I didn't think it would affect her this much.'

The shop owner returned with a glass of cool water, and handed it to Grandma Megan who put the glass to Rosie's lips.

'Just small sips, Rosie love. That's it.'

'I've heard of this happening, but in all the time I've had dealings with crystals, I've never seen such a strong reaction,' said the woman.

Colour was starting to return to Rosie's cheeks, and she attempted to get up off the chair.

Grandma Megan standing by Rosie's side, placed a hand on her grand-daughter's shoulder, and gently pushed her back down.

'Wait a few more minutes dear, before you get up.'

'But I must go back in,' said Rosie. There's something I need!'

'I'll get it for you,' offered Avery. 'Just tell me what it is. My treat.'

He bent down to Rosie, and she whispered in his ear. Avery gave her a searching look, nodded his head and followed the owner of the shop back inside. He went across to a shelf, lifted the crystal in his hand, and then turned and held it up so Rosie could see it. She nodded her head and gave him a beautiful smile.

Avery purchased the item and back outside the shop he presented it with a flourish to Rosie. 'Thank you,' she said, as she accepted the gift.

Grandma Megan stepped across to Avery and whispered, 'You can't afford that!'

'The woman let me have it for half price,' he explained. 'I think she knows it's going to a good home and will be well used, instead of it just sitting on a shelf gathering dust.

They both turned and looked at the shop. Grandma Megan locked eyes with the woman and gave a little nod. The woman was standing at the window watching them. She smiled and lifted a hand.

Grandma Megan, Rosie and Avery then made their way slowly back to Marissa who was waiting patiently for them.

'Well that was eventful,' exclaimed Marissa, as they all climbed into the car.

'You can say that again,' replied Grandma Megan, as she started the engine.

'Won't bother,' answered Marissa, as her engine purred and they slowly made their way towards the exit.

The store owner was still standing in the same place watching them leave. She had a very thoughtful expression on her face.

As soon as they arrived home Rosie went straight up to her bedroom, unwrapped her package and held it lovingly in her hands.

'You are so beautiful and I know we are going to get on very well together,' Rosie said quietly.

Trilby who was sitting on the window sill made Rosie jump by saying, 'Why are you talking to a piece of rock?'

'Oh Trilby, I didn't see you there. This is no ordinary piece of rock. This is a Rainbow Quartz Crystal Ball. Look at all the beautiful colours inside, especially when the sun catches it. And there is a small cone for her to sit on too.'

'Her to sit on. How do you know it's a her?'

'I just know,' answered Rosie. 'I'll have to think of a name for her too.'

'You're getting weirder by the day,' said Trilby. 'Do you know that?'

Rosie chuckled, placed the crystal ball on the little holder and promised she would cleanse it later after her dinner.

'What! You're going to give it a bath too!' exclaimed Trilby.

'No,' laughed Rosie. 'I'll just hold her under clear running water to get rid of any negative energy, and then at the next full moon in a few days' time, I'll sit her in the window for a few nights, and the light of the moon will re-charge her and give her energy.'

Just then Grandma Megan called up the stairs that dinner was ready.

Saved from any more questions, Rosie ran down the stairs and headed for the kitchen.

Bella was waiting for her and gave her a big smile whilst sitting on her little bottom waving her paws in the air.

'Hello Bella,' greeted Rosie, bending down and picking up the little dog to give her a cuddle. 'Has everything been alright with you and Amber?'

'They are all fine,' Grandma Megan assured Rosie. 'Now sit yourself down and eat your dinner. You need to recharge your batteries so to speak. That was quite an outing we had today, one way and another.'

'Where's Uncle Avery?' enquired Rosie. 'I haven't thanked him properly for my gift.'

'He's out in his workshop as usual. I've taken his dinner over to him. He said he couldn't spare any more time away from his latest project, whatever that is. You can thank him after you've eaten. I would also like to have a look at your gift. I haven't seen it properly myself yet.'

'It's beautiful,' enthused Rosie. 'The colours that sparkle inside are so bright and pure, and I'm sure looking deep into it I can make out a tree or two. The more I look the more I see, although I've only done it for a minute or two.'

'It sounds quite powerful to me dear. You'll have to learn how to use it properly.'

'I know,' agreed Rosie. 'I'm sure Juniper, my book of magic, will be a great help with that.'

Their meal finished, they cleared away the dishes and went outside to feed all the animals, making sure they had all they needed for the night.

Whilst Rosie went in search of her Uncle Avery to thank him for her gift, Grandma Megan quickly planted the herbs she had purchased.

Rosie was feeling very tired by now and was ready for her bed.

Whilst all this was going on Trilby was perched up in a nearby tree deep in thought. She could see Rosie was very tired now, and would be fast asleep once she snuggled down in her bed.

Trilby was busy making plans of her own.

Chapter 15

All was peaceful. The animals had settled down for the night, and so had Grandma Megan, Rosie, and Avery.

Trilby was sitting perched on the fence, just outside the barn.

Erin, the silver fox, had been spending the last couple of days resting up in there so he could go out at night, which he preferred to do.

'What's keeping him?' Trilby grumbled to herself.

It had been a very warm summer's day and the night was clear and bright. Because it was still very warm Grandma Megan had decided to leave the barn door open so the animals would get extra air.

After what seemed an age to Trilby, she spotted the silver fox slowly walking out of the barn.

'At last. What kept you so long?' asked Trilby.

'Firstly, I didn't know you were waiting for me, and secondly I fell asleep again after the delicious supper Grandma Megan gave to me. What's up anyway?' enquired Erin.

'I want to enlist your help.' said Trilby.

'Really? I must say I'm surprised,' he replied.

'Now don't be smart,' retorted Trilby.'

'Apologies,' said Erin quietly.

'Accepted. Now I don't know whether you have heard or not, but Rosie's father - who everybody thought was dead, died abroad or something – is being held captive somewhere nearby, and I thought it would be a good idea if we could scout around a bit, and see if we could find any clues. I was going to enlist the help of that gnome chappie, but he's still trying to get the hang of his legs, and I don't think he's stopped eating since he started.'

'What can I do to help,' asked Erin.

'Well, if I fly about looking for clues or see anything I think is odd, I thought you could use that good sense of smell you have, and maybe find anything I miss.'

'Happy to,' he agreed.

'Good. Now, if you find anything you think is out of the ordinary, give a howl, or bark, and I'll come and find you.'

Erin threw back his head and emitted a high-pitched howl.

'That'll do nicely.' acknowledged Trilby. She was glad he had agreed to help in her search because she was determined to find clues, anything to help Rosie rescue her father. Grandma Megan, and Rosie, had been so good to her, and this was one way she hoped to repay them. It seemed too good an opportunity to miss.

'Which way shall we go?' enquired Erin.

'I've been thinking a lot about that and suggest we make for the forest. I doubt that whoever has him will be out in broad daylight or in the open. So, if we head for the thicker part of the forest and hunt around there first. If I find something I'm not sure about I'll come and find you.'

'Off we go then,' said Erin, and loped off in the direction of the forest. 'See you later.'

Trilby took to the air and flew ahead of Erin. She hadn't been too sure whether to trust him or not when she had first met him, but she was rapidly changing her mind.

Flitting from tree to tree Trilby was on the alert for anything that seemed out of place or odd. She hadn't noticed anything at all after some time, and was just wondering how Erin was getting on and whether he was nearby, when she heard a high-pitched howl.

Her head shot up from where she was looking closely at some vegetation, and she quickly locked on to the direction the howl had come from.

Taking to the air she soon spotted Erin who was sitting on the forest floor waiting for her. He was looking intently at something in front of him.

'What have you found?' asked Trilby landing on a nearby branch.

'Look at that,' instructed Erin, indicating the forest floor in front of him.

'What? I can't see anything.'

'Then it's a good thing you asked for my help isn't it,' chuckled Erin.

'Now don't get too big for your paws,' she retorted. Trilby didn't like being shown up as dumb.

'Ok.' Erin then explained. 'I just think it's strange that a wheelbarrow has recently been pushed along this path. Why would that be? I can smell two sets of footprints, and whatever was in said wheelbarrow must have been heavy, and hard to push by the look of the trail left behind. It's quite deep where the ground is very damp and doesn't get much sun to dry it out with the thick canopy of the trees.'

'You're right!' she exclaimed. 'I should have seen that some way back.' She wasn't going to admit that she hadn't had a clue what she was looking for. 'What should we do now?'

'I think we should follow the tracks and see where they take us. We haven't found anything else odd, and we've nothing to lose if it leads to a dead end. But we must investigate.'

'Quite right,' agreed Trilby. 'Exciting, isn't it?'

'Mmmmm' rumbled Erin, as he slowly walked along with his nose close to the ground.

After ten minutes or so of silently following the signs, Erin stopped and sat down.

'What's up?' enquired Trilby. 'Not tired, are you?'

They were in front of a couple of extra large trees, taller and much thicker than the others.

'That's very weird, and no I'm not tired. Do you need spectacles Trilby? Can't you see anything peculiar?'

'My eyes are fine, thank you very much, and no I can't see anything peculiar as you put it. I'm just not as accomplished at this tracking thing as you are. What can you see now?'

'It's what I can't see. The trail stops here. It doesn't go around the trees or anywhere else as far as I can see.'

'But it can't have just vanished!' Trilby exclaimed. 'We were doing so well too.'

Getting to his feet and sniffing around, Erin had to admit this had beaten him. He had never come across anything like it before.

Trilby flew down from the branch she had been sitting on, and stood beside Erin.

'Do you know what I think?' she asked. 'I think there's some magic afoot here, and we need to let Grandma Megan know what we've found. We can't do anything ourselves. It's much too strong a magic for me to try anything. I suggest we return to the cottage and wait for Rosie, and Grandma Megan, to get up and start their day.'

Erin agreed. Trilby had grown weary over the time they had been searching, it seemed like most of the night to her, and so Erin happily agreed to give her a ride. Sitting on his neck and gripping his thick coat, they both headed back to the cottage taking the shortest route.

Chapter 16

Avery was up bright and early. He loved the summer mornings with the early dawn, and it gave him so much more daylight to work on his inventions.

This morning he was standing at his workshop door, a mug in one hand enjoying his first cup of tea of the day and admiring the colours in the sky. He took another mouthful of tea and was so startled at the sight before him, he coughed, spluttered, and most of the drink shot out of his mouth spraying all before him. Pulling a handkerchief out from his trousers pocket, and mopping the front of his shirt, he muttered, 'Well I never.'

Thinking he shouldn't really be surprised these days at what went on here. But he never expected to see this. The little faery was riding on Erin's shoulders, and both were looking as thick as thieves.

'I hope they haven't been up to anything they shouldn't,' he mumbled.

Erin sauntered into the barn and laid down on some nice clean straw, whilst Trilby made herself comfortable sitting on the sweet hay in Hector's hay net. They both settled down to wait patiently although this was difficult for Trilby because the hay kept tickling her, making her fidget. This annoyed Hector and he kicked out with a back leg saying, 'Keep still, it's much too early to get up yet.'

'Ok, ok,' said Trilby. 'How can you eat this stuff, it's so dry and itchy.'

'Go and annoy someone else then,' grumbled Hector.

'No, it's alright, I think I'm comfy now.'

'Thank goodness,' said Hector, and closing his eyes he drifted off to sleep again.

Chapter 17

Jack and Charlie, always early risers, were in the forest again checking the traps to see if they had caught anything overnight. Two of the traps had dead rabbits in them but the rest were empty.

'Mum will be pleased with these,' said Jack. 'Rabbit for dinner tonight I think.'

Turning to make their way back to their gypsy camp for some breakfast, Charlie gave a delighted shout of 'Yes!' and ran off to the left.

'What's up with you?' asked Jack, surprised at seeing his mate sprinting off like that.

He knew there weren't any more of their traps in this area, so it couldn't be that. He followed at a run anyway.

Charlie was on his hands and knees at the base of a tree, scraping away freshly disturbed soil and leaves. They were in a part of the forest that wasn't too dense, and the early morning sun was filtering through the branches.

'What are you doing?' asked Jack.

Charlie sat back on his haunches and carefully brushed some dirt and leaves from the object in his hands. He held it up for Jack to see.

'How did you know that was there?' demanded Jack.

'I didn't,' replied Charlie, who now had a huge grin on his face. I saw the sun glinting on something and came to check it out. Do you think it's another part of the treasure the golden acorn belonged to?'

'I don't know, but it seems weird to me that it's stuffed down a rabbit hole. This hole is obviously in use, judging by the fresh soil around about.'

'Maybe it wasn't in use when this was buried, but the rabbit decided to make use of it, and dislodged this when digging down.'

'Maybe,' mused Jack. 'Seems funny though, to put a piece here and a piece there. The bit I found, the golden acorn, was on top of some green bush if you remember.'

'Whatever,' replied Charlie. 'I've found a piece of the treasure. This is great. Any idea what it is?'

Jack held out his hand. 'Let me have a closer look.'

Charlie got to his feet and passed the object across to Jack who turned it around in his hands and smoothed it with both thumbs. It looks like some sort of cup, but what it's for I haven't the foggiest. I'm sure it's silver though, and it can't have been here very long cos it's bright and shiny and silver goes a weird colour when not polished.'

Charlie held out his hand for Jack to give it back to him. He was a little worried that his mate would start tossing it into the air and catching it, like he had done with the golden acorn, and look what had happened to that. One minute it was there and the next, gone.

Handing it back Jack, asked 'What are you going to do with it?'

'Don't know yet. But we've found two pieces now, maybe we'll find more. Shall we keep looking?'

'Maybe later. We know where you found this and I'm hungry. That warden chap might appear soon too, and I don't want to meet him with two rabbits on me.

'Good thinking,' agreed Charlie, carefully placing the silver cup in one of his large pockets. Before we go though, let me just check to make sure there isn't anything else down there.'

Getting back down on his hands and knees he stuck his hand gingerly into the rabbit hole. It went quite a long way down and the whole of his arm was now inside when Jack bent down, poked Charlie in his ribs and shouted 'Boo', in his left ear.

'Aaahhh!' shrieked Charlie pulling his arm back out of the hole quickly, and jumping to his feet.

'Whatcha do that for?' he demanded.

'Just seemed like a good idea at the time,' replied Jack, and laughing at Charlie's scared expression he turned and started walking away before Charlie clouted him.

'I don't think that was very funny. Me heart's about to jump out of me chest.'

'Nothing else in there then,' said Jack, still smiling.

'No, nothing else,' answered Charlie, and they both headed off in the direction of their camp. Charlie had one hand inside his large pocket holding on to the silver cup.

Chapter 18

That same morning, Grandma Megan was in the back garden feeding her chickens, and chattering away to them as she usually did. Rupert the young rooster had been practising his early morning call so often the day before, he had given himself a sore throat. Finished with scattering their seed, Grandma Megan bent down and scooped Rupert up into her arms. 'I have something nice here for you, young man,' she said, soothingly to Rupert. She was so busy syringing cough syrup down his throat, she got quite a start when Trilby started fluttering around her head chattering very fast in her excitement.

Erin just sat to one side and let her get on with it.

'Trilby, wait a minute until I've finished giving Rupert his medicine,' she admonished the little faery. 'Then I'm all ears.'

She squirted a little more syrup into Rupert's beak, which made is eyes water, but satisfied most of it had gone down, Grandma Megan placed the little rooster back onto the ground and watched him strut off to get his breakfast, noticing as he did so that Rupert now had the hic-cups.

'That should do the trick,' she said. Then focusing on Trilby, she asked, 'Now, what's up?'

The silver fox started to speak, but Trilby got in first and shouted, which wasn't all that loud, since she was only a little faery.

'We've been investigating.'

'Have you now,' said Grandma Megan. 'What and where have you been investigating?'

Trilby then went on to explain all they had found out the night before.

Grandma Megan was very surprised to say the least, and looked across to where Erin was still sitting. He nodded his head and said, 'It's true. Once the trail vanished we came back here to wait for you to get up.'

'Well I never. That's very good work on both your parts,' she acknowledged. 'I think we'd better contact Bertrum in the elf village, and let him know. 'Come along and we'll use Mira the mirror straight away. She hasn't been used so much in ages. It's a good thing Bertrum insisted I had some form of communication.'

'We'll come with you,' volunteered Trilby, looking across at Erin who nodded in agreement. 'Just in case he needs extra information,' continued Trilby.

WHOOMPH!

'Aaahhh, not again,' moaned Grandma Megan as she involuntarily ducked down. Trilby flew to Grandma Megan and dived inside her pinafore pocket for safety, whilst Erin bolted inside the barn and hid under a pile of straw.

'What on earth is Avery up to now? I thought all that nonsense was finished with,' grumbled Grandma Megan, as she straightened up and stood watching all the animals scattering in all directions.

Rupert, the rooster had feinted with shock. He hadn't been at the homestead when the explosions occurred weeks before, so it was much more of a shock for him. But it still scared the life out of one and all.

Grandma Megan strode across and gently picked Rupert up, and cradled him in her arms. She turned and looked across to Avery's workshop. Luckily the door hadn't been blown off this time, and Avery stood there looking out at them all. His face was blackened, and all his hair was standing up on end, more so than usual.

'Sorry Megan, quite unexpected,' he called out to her.

'Mmmmm. What are you up to this time?'

'Can't say, it's a secret,' said Avery.

'Well do try and stop frightening one and all, will you? There's a good chap.'

Avery lifted his hand in acknowledgement, and disappeared back inside his workshop.

'Right let's try and get back indoors now, shall we? Poor Rupert here is in a dead feint.'

Walking back into the kitchen, Trilby now fluttering close to Grandma Megan's head, and Erin back out of the barn was trotting by her side but still looking behind him.

Grandma Megan headed straight for her large kitchen dresser, opened a small cupboard and lifted out a little white jar of her homemade smelling salts. Taking this across and placing it on the table, she then sat down and placed Rupert on her lap. Unscrewing the lid from the jar and placing it on the table she scooped a little of the mixture onto a finger and held it under Rupert's beak for only a few seconds. Nothing happened. Grandma Megan did the same again with the mixture on her finger.

'Is he dead?' enquired Trilby.

At that moment Rupert gave a little croak and opened his eyes.

'He's boss-eyed!' cried Trilby, who was watching him very closely.

'Let's just wait a little while,' suggested Grandma Megan. Give him time.'

Sure enough, Rupert then blinked his eyes a few, and gazed up at Grandma Megan.

'It's alright little chap,' she whispered to him. 'You've just had a nasty fright but you'll be right as rain shortly. Grandma Megan, stood up and slowly carried Rupert to the back door to let him see all was well, and to breathe in some fresh air. She then bent down and placed the little rooster onto the ground. He fluffed up his feathers and slowly walked off, a little unsteadily.

'Ha! He walks just like the gnome now,' laughed Trilby.

'Come back inside Trilby. We need to contact Oakenveil quickly.'

'Where's Rosie,' asked Trilby.

'She's up in her room studying,' replied Grandma Megan. 'I took her breakfast up to her earlier and she was working hard, so we must leave her to it for the time being.'

'But we must tell her what we've found,' said Trilby.

'No, we'll leave her for now. She'll only want to chase off and see for herself, and as she has her mind on her studies, at least that's keeping her occupied.'

Whilst she had been replying to Trilby, Grandma Megan had retrieved Mira from the back of the drawer and placed her on the table. Gently rubbing the frame, it wasn't long before Rowena appeared. After relaying to Rowena. the details of what Trilby and Erin had found the night before, it was agreed that Bertrum, would meet Erin at Cornelius later that evening and Erin would show him where the trail disappeared.

'What about me, I was there too,' said Trilby, a little petulantly.

'I know you were Trilby dear, but I need you here to make sure Rosie doesn't go off investigating herself again, and if she does, then I rely on you to keep looking after her and making sure she's safe.'

Pacified, Trilby reluctantly agreed. Then she said, 'I don't understand why it's taking so long, and why we can't just storm in and rescue him, wherever he is.'

'That would be much too dangerous,' said Grandma Megan. 'The elves, and Rosie's father, might be injured, and we don't want that to happen now do we?'

'Suppose not,' agreed Trilby.

Chapter 19

Wolfric was just finishing tidying up his father's workshop. He used a corner of the workshop and his father's tools when he had a certain project to do, and so it was only fair he kept the place clean and tidy.

He had been working hard on his school project, and his flute was almost finished. He decided now was the right time to put it aside for a few days, and come back to it with a fresh eye. Then he would put the finishing touches to it.

Bertrum was very pleased with his son's progress, and the evening before had given Wolfric permission to go and visit Grandma Megan, and Rosie. He was really looking forward to seeing them again, provided Cornelius confirmed the coast was clear, and the door of the great old oak tree could be opened.

Looking about him and checking all was clean and tidy, he closed and locked the workshop door. He went and popped his head inside his home beside the workshop and called goodbye to his mother, then happily made his way down the lane and through the tunnel leading to Cornelius.

Arriving at the door, he reached up and rang the bell to alert Cornelius someone was waiting.

Cornelius spent a lot of time sleeping nowadays. It was nearing the time when he had to have his life enhancing elixir. As he was hundreds of years old it was to be expected really.

The little bell tinkled merrily. A loud clang would have given Cornelius too much of a shock, especially if he was dozing.

'Well if it isn't young Wolfric,' greeted the great old oak, after clearing his throat.

'Hello Cornelius. How are you?' greeted Wolfric.

'Oh, so so, you know. Mustn't grumble.'

'Is it safe to open the door?' enquired Wolfric

After what seemed an age to Wolfric, Cornelius mumbled, 'All clear,' and silently opened the little door just far enough for Wolfric to slip through.

'Thank you,' said Wolfric, and was just about to sprint off when the old tree said,

'Hold on young'un, have....?'

'Yes Cornelius, I have the key to get back in, and I'll keep it safe,' answered Wolfric, knowing what the great old oak was going to ask him, and then laughing and raising a hand in farewell he made a quick dash across the glade into the forest.

Chuckling his deep chuckle, Cornelius closed the door and faded from view.

Wolfric loved this forest and all the animals living in it. He swiftly made his way to the outskirts, and reached the one-hundred-acre field that skirted Grandma Megan's homestead. He was careful also to keep a watchful eye all around making sure he did not meet Fred Bennett, the warden or anyone else who may be wandering about.

In no time at all he was entering the back gate. Hector the new forest pony saw him arrive and gave him a cheerful whinny in greeting. Probably hoping Wolfric would ride him again, and he could show off some of his fanciful moves.

Bella, ever vigilant, ran to meet him and gave him a lovely smile and one of her little barks to let Grandma Megan know they had a visitor.

'Wolfric, my dear, what a lovely surprise,' greeted Grandma Megan, appearing at the kitchen door. 'Come along in. Rosie will be thrilled to see you. She's been upstairs too long studying, so I think it's about time she had a break.'

School work?' enquired Wolfric.

'Some work for school, although I'm pretty sure she's on top of that now, but she has various other studies to do because she is who she is. It's an awful lot for a young girl just turned twelve years, but she seems to be coping, and I think she is enjoying most of it. It's just the worry of her father that gets her down, understandably.'

'What other studies does she have?' enquired Wolfric, confused.

'I'll let her tell you herself when she's ready dear. Sit yourself down and I'll go and let her know you're here.'

Grandma Megan made her way up the stairs to Rosie's bedroom. Rosie usually worked in the dining-room where her bookcase with desk combined, had pride of place. Avery had handmade this for Rosie's last birthday. and it was decorated with an inlay of all manner of birds, butterflies and small mammals that Rosie loved. Rosie adored this piece of furniture, but every so often, when she had certain other studies to do. she preferred her bedroom with the crystals at the window, the view, and the peaceful feeling of the room.

This morning, she was working with Juniper, the very old book of magic, and her crystal ball, recently named Selima.

Rosie's bedroom door was open, so Grandma Megan stood for a few moments watching her grand-daughter who was sitting cross legged on her bed with books all around her. She was chattering away to Juniper, and consulting Selima.

'Well I never!' Grandma Megan exclaimed surprised. 'That's amazing.'

Spotting her grandma waiting patiently in the doorway, Rosie gave her a big smile.

'Is it all going well dear?' enquired Grandma Megan.

'Yes, it is, thank you. I seem to be getting the hang of it, although Juniper lets me know if I'm making a hash of things,' she said laughing. 'Would you like to know what I've been working on?'

'I would be very interested to hear all about it, but at this moment we have a visitor downstairs.'

'Have we? Who?'

'Wolfric. He was wondering whether you fancied going for a walk with him. I think the fresh air would do you good my dear,' said Grandma Megan.

'Brilliant,' exclaimed Rosie, jumping off the bed, and making a dash for the door. Grandma Megan put out an arm to stop her dashing through, and down the stairs.

Rosie looked enquiringly at her grandma.

'Haven't you forgotten something,' said Grandma Megan, looking pointedly at the bed, especially at the old book of magic.

'Oh, but I thought he would be safe there,' said Rosie.

'Now, you must remember what Avery said when you first received Juniper. He must never fall into the wrong hands. That would be disastrous. So, I think to be on the safe side, you must make it a habit to put him away in his secret compartment when you've finished.'

'Sorry Grandma.'

Rosie went across to her bed, closed the book of magic and carefully picked him up and carried him down the stairs. Entering the dining-room she knelt, opened the secret compartment in her bookcase cum desk, and securely closed the little door.

'Good girl. It's better to be safe than sorry,' said Grandma Megan. 'Now come along. I'm sure Wolfric is wondering where we've got to.'

'Hello Wolfric,' greeted Rosie, as she entered the kitchen. 'This is a very welcome surprise.'

'Hello Rosie, I'm having a break from my own project today, and wondered whether you'd like to go for a walk in this lovely sunshine?'

'Sounds a good idea to me,' agreed Rosie.

'Just what the doctor ordered,' agreed Grandma Megan, happy Wolfric had arrived. 'What about taking Bella out for a nice walk with you. She has been so good these weeks looking after that little kitten, and I'm sure she wouldn't say no. Amber is quite independent now although she still looks for reassurance from Bella at night.'

Rosie turned to Bella and asked, 'Would you like to come with us Bella?'

The little dog sat on her haunches and waved her little paws in the air, giving a big smile at the same time.

'They all laughed, and Grandma Megan said, 'That's settled then. Off you all go and have a lovely time.'

Bella raced out of the door, down the path and waited for Rosie, and Wolfric, to follow her and open the gate. Once out of the gate she bounded around in the one-hundred-acre field enjoying her freedom, and finding all sorts of wonderful smells.

'Whilst I was waiting for you in the kitchen, I thought I was seeing things, but I'm sure there was a little gnome there. Trilby was with him, and badgering him to do something he was having some difficulty with,' said Wolfric.

Rosie laughed. 'You weren't seeing things. Trilby decided we might need some extra help rescuing my father. She thought it wasn't right for the little garden gnome to stand around all day doing nothing. So, she used some faery magic, brought him to life and the poor little man is having a hard time trying to get to grips with walking etc. I'm afraid patience is not one of Trilby's virtues.'

'Oh, I see. Now, where shall we go?

'Well, I'm curious about something I saw in my crystal. I'd like to check it out, although I'm not sure where it might be.'

'What crystal?'

'Oh, that reminds me, I have some sweets for you back at the cottage. Grandma Megan, Uncle Avery, and myself, went to the funfair the other day, and had a great time, Anyway, on the way home we stopped at a little place with a crystal shop. Uncle Avery bought me a gift of a gorgeous rainbow crystal ball, and I can see various things when looking at it.' Rosie decided she wouldn't mention she'd had a funny turn in the shop.

'So, what do you want to check out?'

'It showed me two very large trees for some reason. I've seen them more than once, and that made me think it's significant for some reason,' said Rosie.

Bella was keeping up with them. She wasn't letting them out of her sight now they had entered the forest. She was still enjoying herself sniffing here and there and bounding around, but careful not to stray far.

'Did you see anything else that might indicate where these trees might be?'

'Not really, just that they're really large. All the other ones around them, although they're tall, are much thinner and not quite so close together,' said Rosie.

'Well, let's have a walk around and we might spot something,' suggested Wolfric. 'Bella's enjoying herself, and it is lovely being out and about again.

Sauntering along, they found some late wild strawberries, and enjoyed the fresh sweetness.

'Elmo would be really jealous if he knew we'd found these,' said Wolfric, popping another strawberry into his mouth. 'He just loves fruit.' Elmo is the little house Brownie who lives with Wolfric and his family.

Rosie then asked after Elmo, and the rest of his family. They were just sauntering along when Rosie suddenly looked to her left, and stopped in her tracks.

'There they are!' she exclaimed, pointing her finger. 'Look, just as I saw them in the crystal.'

Wolfric looked in the direction Rosie was pointing, and had to agree they looked just as she had described them earlier.

'Let's have a closer look,' said Rosie, walking towards the trees.

Wolfric followed, but he started to have a bad feeling about this spot. 'Careful Rosie. We don't know what we're walking into,' he warned.

'Don't be silly, it's just part of the forest,' she replied, looking back over her shoulder.

Wolfric, ever watchful, scooped up Bella who was sniffing around in front of him, and then he shot forward, grabbed Rosie by her left arm, and pulled her to his side behind a large holly bush.

She was very surprised, and was just about to ask indignantly what he was doing, when he placed an index finger to his lips and urged her to be quiet. Then, keeping hold of Bella, he carefully parted some of the holly in front of them so they could both see what was going on.

Two strange individuals were now standing in front of the large trees that Rosie had been walking towards. One was very tall and thin, wearing a black pointed hat and black cloak. The other was short and dumpy, but dressed in the same form of clothing. They seemed to be arguing about something, but were speaking so quietly Rosie, and Wolfric, couldn't hear what was being said.

Bella started to struggle and whimper wanting to get down and continue her exploring, so Wolfric passed her across to Rosie to try and keep her quiet.

'Shush Bella,' Rosie whispered. 'You can get down in a little while, but you must stay quiet. We don't want to be seen. Bella seemed to understand and stayed calm and quiet.

'What was that?' asked the taller of the two. 'I swear I heard something. Who's there?' he called out.

Rosie, and Wolfric, hardly dared to breath.

'Nothing. Probably just some animal in the woods,' said the dumpy one. 'You're getting paranoid.'

'No, I'm not. I'm just being careful, which is what you should do more of. We have a lot to lose here, and you know what will happen if we fail.'

'I know, I know,' grumbled the dumpy one. 'But this has been going on and on, and I'm getting fed up with it.'

'It won't be for much longer I'm sure. We are so close now. We daren't upset the high priestess.

'I know,' replied the dumpy one giving a shiver. 'Doesn't bear thinking about.'

'Well, come on then, we'd better not hang around here,' and he urged the dumpy one ahead of him with a push or two.

Rosie, and Wolfric, watched the pair swiftly walk away.

'What do you think that was all about?' asked Rosie, looking at Wolfric. 'Have you seen those two before? Do you know who they are?'

Wolfric shook his head. 'No, I've never seen them before. Funny sort of clothes they were wearing though.'

'Have they gone? Let's get closer and have a look around.'

Wolfric wasn't too keen to do this, but the bad feeling he'd had earlier had gone, so he agreed to have a quick look.

'Put Bella down now and she can have a hunt around too. If there is anything she doesn't like her hackles will rise, so keep an eye on her and stay ready to run if necessary,' said Wolfric, looking all around.

Gently placing Bella on the ground, Rosie slowly moved out from where they had been hiding, and headed towards the two large trees. Bella, was trotting by her side, and Wolfric was moving slightly ahead of them looking this way and that, keeping his eyes peeled, every sense alert.

Bella didn't show any signs of distress and they reached the trees without incident. Both trees were huge and most of their bark was covered in thick ivy. They walked around the trees but on first inspection didn't notice anything out of the ordinary.

Reaching the spot where they had seen the two characters standing, Rosie put her hand on the nearest tree, and looked at Wolfric.

'I don't know whether it's my nerves, but I'm sure I can feel a vibration of sorts,' said Rosie.

Wolfric placed his hand next to Rosie's, and he nodded his head. 'You're right, I can feel it too.'

'Let's try and move some of the ivy, see if there's anything underneath.

They both tugged and pushed, but the ivy was very thick and the stems had roots that anchored themselves well and truly into the bark making it almost impossible to move. Rosie lifted a leg and put her foot against the trunk to give herself extra pulling power. It did help a little but her hands slipped and she ended up falling backwards, landing on her rump.

'I'm sure there must be a way in,' she said, getting to her feet and rubbing her bottom.

'There is some strong magic here I think, said Wolfric. 'I think the best thing is to let my father know what we have found.'

'That sounds like a good idea, and I'll go back and consult the old book of magic and my new crystal. After all the crystal did show me the trees, so maybe I need to look harder and it might show me something else.'

Turning to see where Bella was, Wolfric caught his right foot under some of the ivy trailing across the ground, and felt himself falling. He put out his hands in front of him to try and break his fall, but still slammed against the tree trunk with some force.

Grrrumph!

'What was that noise?' said Rosie, trying to keep her voice from trembling. 'You haven't broken any bones, have you?'

'No, no bones broken, just a bit winded,' said Wolfric, getting to his feet and moving closer to inspect the tree he had fallen against.

'Rosie look! This seems to be a way in. It doesn't open very far, but it's definitely an opening.'

Rosie moved to his side and peered in. 'It's very dark in there. What was it you pushed when you fell?'

'I tried to hang on to something to stop my fall, so it could be anything.'

They felt all around when suddenly Rosie said in a small voice, 'I think I've found it. Look at this.'

There was a lever of sorts, and to camouflage it the ivy had been wound round and round and knotted. Anyone just looking over the tree trunk would never have spotted it.

'Very clever,' said Wolfric. 'Do we go in?'

'Well, we've come this far, so it would be silly not to, I suppose,' said Rosie.

Wolfric entered first with Rosie close behind. There was a sudden click and the door snapped shut.

'Nooo,' cried Rosie. 'We might be trapped now, and poor little Bella is still outside. What made it shut like that?'

'We must have triggered something,' said Wolfric. 'Come on, let's see where this leads to. I'm sure Bella will find her way back home.'

Reluctant to do so, Rosie turned and followed Wolfric. He led the way down a slope which brought them to a long passageway. It was dark and creepy, but luckily Wolfric had a small torch in one of his pockets, so at least they had a little light.

Outside Bella couldn't understand why she had been left behind, and sat barking at the trees. She had been so busy sniffing around she hadn't seen where Rosie, and Wolfric, had gone. Feeling frightened now, she turned and ran. All she knew was that her mistress had disappeared, and she had to get back to Grandma Megan as soon as she could.

Running as fast as her little legs would allow, she raced along paths, jumped brambles, ferns and small bushes, nearly tripping up Fred Bennett, in the process of cutting across him and heading for the one-hundred-acre field.

'Well I never,' breathed Fred Bennett. 'If I'm not mistaken that was Bella, Rosie's little dog. It's not like her to be out on her own.' He stood there looking about him and listening, expecting to see Rosie running after her, but all was silent.

Bella reached the little gate at the cottage and stood there barking. Grandma Megan ran to the kitchen door wondering what the noise was all about. Opening the gate, she was astonished to see Bella on her own, jumping up and down, and barking in an agitated state trying to tell Grandma Megan what had happened.

Grandma Megan bent down, picked up the little dog, and called to Avery.

Avery had heard the commotion and come to his workshop door. 'What's all the noise about?' he asked. 'It's not like Bella to carry on like that.'

'I know it's not, but she's come back on her own. Rosie, and Wolfric, took her out for a walk over an hour ago, but Bella has returned on her own. Rosie would never let her do that.'

'Come,' said Avery. 'Let's find Trilby. I take it she's still here because Rosie went out with Wolfric.'

'Yes, I think she's in the barn. She's quite taken with Erin, and spends part of the day with him hoping to do more investigating.'

'Well she should be able to tell us what Bella is trying to say.'

Normally Grandma Megan would understand what the little dog was saying, but this was so garbled and Bella was so excited, she was muddling things up.

They headed for the barn, Grandma Megan still carrying Bella who was a little calmer now.

'Trilby,' called out Grandma Megan, when they entered.

'I didn't do it,' said Trilby in reply.

Grandma Megan ignored this and said, 'Trilby we need your help. Bella here is trying to tell us something, and we can't understand what it is.' She lowered Bella onto the ground.

'Probably asking for a bone or something.'

'No dear, this is quite serious. Rosie, and Wolfric, took her out for a walk and only Bella has returned.'

'WHAT!'

'Please listen to what Bella is trying to say.'

Bella was sitting on the ground panting.

'Well, first I think she needs a drink of water, she's run a long way,' said Trilby.

'Oh right,' said Avery, and went to fetch a bowl of water.

Bella had a long drink, and then started her barking again, although it wasn't quite as frantic as before, and there were some whines and little noises at the end.

'Cripes,' said Trilby, and then relayed all Bella had told her.

'B-But they can't have just disappeared like that,' spluttered Grandma Megan.

'It sounds like the two large trees Erin, and I came to a dead end at,' said Trilby.

'Yes, it does,' admitted Erin. 'Well, I'll be meeting Bertrum, later this evening, and we'll be checking that particular place out thoroughly.'

'I wish I could come too,' sighed Trilby.

'You can if you want to, as Rosie isn't here for you to keep an eye on,' agreed Grandma Megan.

'No, I'd rather not go with Bertrum,' said Trilby screwing up her face.

Grandma Megan nodded her head. She knew Trilby was worried she would be taken back and locked in the toy store in Oakenveil again.

'You stay here with me Trilby, dear,' said Grandma Megan.

Once Bella knew she had been understood, and something was going to be done to find her mistress, she returned to the kitchen and snuggled down in her basket with Amber. Amber was slowly returning to her proper colour now, and looked more like the ginger tabby instead of the pink and purple colour Trilby had given her when she was experimenting to see whether she could still change the colour of things. Trilby being an autumn faery, changes the summer leaves of the trees and bushes to their autumn colours.

'That's settled then,' said Grandma Megan. 'All we can do is wait, and see what Bertrum, and Erin, discover this evening. You never know, Rosie and Wolfric might return before then,' she said, hoping this would be the case.

Chapter 20

Whoomph!

'Not again,' shouted Grandma Megan, as one and all dived for cover. The loud explosions were always unexpected and impossible to get used to. Unfortunately, Fred Bennett. the warden, was nearing Grandma Megan's cottage at the time, and heard the full blast himself. As Grandma Megan's cottage is quite a way from the nearest village they had been fortunate so far that they hadn't received complaints from any of the neighbours.

'Oh no,' Grandma Megan groaned. 'That's all we need.'

'Fred Bennett was running as fast as he could towards the cottage, shouting as he did so, 'Quick inside everyone, we're under attack.' He was holding his gun out in front of him at the ready. He vaulted the garden gate, which amazed Grandma Megan, because Fred was in no way a youngster. He was still bending low and grabbed Grandma Megan by her arm to drag her into her kitchen, when she managed to say, 'It's alright Fred, it's only Avery in his workshop inventing something or other.'

'What! Does that often happen? The explosions I mean. I'd be a nervous wreck and have no hair left at all, if I lived here.'

'Well, we've had a fairly long period of peace and quiet, but it has been getting noisy again I'm afraid. He won't tell me what he's inventing this time, says it's a secret.'

'I see,' said Fred, standing up straight and releasing Grandma Megan's arm. 'Shall I go and see him, see what he's up to?'

'Oh no, please don't do that. He's always very sorry, and he doesn't like anyone entering his domain as he calls it.'

'If you say so,' said Fred.

'Now, did you want to see me about anything?' asked Grandma Megan.

'Well yes, as a matter of fact I did. I was rather surprised earlier to see little Bella tearing through the forest on her own. She looked quite distressed, not her usual self at all. I came to see if everything is alright, and to ask how Rosie is doing.'

'Oh, they are both fine, thank you Fred. I expect Bella thought that she had left the little kitten too long, and was racing back to see to her. You know she's been looking after the little orphan so well, and today was the first day she'd gone out for a nice walk since Amber was found in the barn.'

Grandma Megan was standing facing Fred, and to her relief she could see Trilby on the nearby fence behind Fred. Taking Fred's arm, she steered him towards her vegetable garden, at the same time behind Fred's back she motioned for Trilby to get to the kitchen and hide Cyan.

'Come and see how well the peas and carrots have done this year. You haven't been to see us for a while, and I'm sure you'll be surprised how they have come on. Maybe you would like to take some home with you,' said Grandma Megan.

'Very kind, very kind,' said Fred. He did like coming to Grandma Megan's, because he never left empty handed. Pots of jam, or pickle, a cake, all manner of goodies that Grandma Megan made herself, and everything she made had that special something to it the locals couldn't quite put their finger on, but loved every morsel none the same.

Grandma Megan picked up a small basket which she kept beside the vegetable patch ready for when she wanted to collect some of the fresh vegetables. 'Then we'll pop in for a cup of tea, which I'm sure you could do with after your fright,' she said. 'And you can see Bella for yourself,' she continued.

'Lovely, lovely,' agreed Fred, walking beside Grandma Megan. Fred tended to repeat things he said.

After gathering enough peas and carrots, they made their way towards the kitchen. Grandma Megan was silently praying Trilby had managed to get Cyan into the back room without too much bother.

Breathing a sigh of relief, Grandma Megan saw all was neat and tidy when they entered, and Bella was lying peacefully in her bed with Amber.

'I see Bella is happy now that she's back with her charge,' said Fred, motioning to the little dog. 'She really takes her job seriously, doesn't she?' said Fred. 'Where's Rosie then?'

'Oh, I expect she's about somewhere. You know these youngsters, always up to something.'

'Very true, very true,' agreed Fred.

'Sit yourself down Fred, and I'll make us a nice pot of tea. Would you like some cake too?' asked Grandma Megan, taking a tin down from the cupboard.

'Splendid, splendid.' Fred like everyone else always felt very happy after Grandma Megan's cooking.

He took off his hat, placed it on his knee and stood his rifle behind him against the wall.

Trilby seemed to be doing a splendid job keeping Cyan quiet, thought Grandma Megan, as she busied herself making the tea and cutting slices of cake. Goodness knows what Fred would think if he saw a garden gnome sitting at the table eating and drinking, and maybe talking to the dog.

'Have some more cake Fred,' said Grandma Megan, seeing he'd almost finished his slice.

'Mmmm, don't mind if I do,' he said, ramming the remaining piece into his mouth. 'Very good cake this,' he managed with a full mouth, although he did spit a few bits out in the process.

'I'm glad you're enjoying it. Maybe you'd like to take the rest home to Ivy as well?'

Fred's mouth was much too full to answer, so he just nodded and gave a crumby smile.

'I'll just put your veggies into a bag, and the rest of the cake into a tin, whilst you're enjoying your cuppa,' said Grandma Megan, fishing into a draw in the dresser for a paper bag.

This done she sat down at the table, and they chatted about things generally for another ten minutes or so.

'Well, I think I must be off now,' said Fred, rising from the table. He placed his hat back on his head, and turning picked up his rifle. 'Thank you, thank you, for your hospitality and the goodies.'

'You are very welcome Fred,' said Grandma Megan, walking with him to the door, and handing him the cake tin and the bag of carrots and peas.

Fred made his way down the path to the gate opened it and passed through. Closing the gate behind him he lifted his hat in farewell, and clutching his goodies, happily went on his way.

Grandma Megan went to let Trilby know the coast was clear.

'That could have been rather tricky to explain, if Fred had seen Cyan,' laughed Grandma Megan. 'Thank you, Trilby dear, for acting so quickly.'

'It's a good job the gnome is getting used to his legs,' said Trilby. 'He can move quite quickly now if he has to. Mind you, if he doesn't cut down on his eating, we'll have to roll him along or pull him on skates or something, He's putting on some weight if you haven't noticed.'

'Oh, he'll slow down soon enough. It's a novelty for him. Maybe if we found something for him to do to keep him occupied,' mused Grandma Megan.

'Excuse me, but I am here you know, and I can hear everything you say,' said Cyan as he waddled out of the back room into the kitchen. He was holding a piece of toast and jam in one hand and an apple in the other,

'It's a good job he's only got two hands,' said Trilby, looking at him.

'I've got pockets,' said Cyan, smiling.

Chapter 21

Rosie, and Wolfric, were still walking down the underground passageway.

'This seems to be going for miles,' grumbled Rosie. 'Surely it must come out somewhere soon.'

'Maybe we missed a door or something. There hasn't been another passage, we would have seen it,' said Wolfric, looking from side to side and behind him.

Rosie was worried about Bella, and hoped she had had the sense to run back to her grandma's cottage.

'We can't just keep walking like this,' said Rosie. She was getting slower and slower.

'I don't see we have much choice,' replied Wolfric.

'Stick your fingers in your ears, Wolfric. I'm going to try something,' said Rosie.

Giving Rosie a quizzical look, Wolfric did as she asked and stuck an index finger in each ear.

Rosie put two fingers into her mouth and blew a piercing whistle.

Wolfric was surprised to say the least. 'Well you seem to have the hang of that now,' he chuckled.

Rosie smiled. 'I did some practice in the back field away from the cottage, so as not to upset the animals,' she explained. 'Just to make sure, I'll send out two signals.'

'What do you mean, signals,' asked Wolfric.

'You can't have forgotten,' said Rosie. 'Oonie said if ever I needed him, then all I had to do was whistle and he would be there.'

'Yes, I know, but we're underground and goodness knows where,' said Wolfric.

'Oh, ye of little faith,' chided Rosie. 'Put your fingers back into your ears, unless you want me to deafen you.'

Wolfric did so and Rosie whistled even louder this time.

They waited a short while and then Rosie whispered, 'Mobie Dickens, it worked. *Look!*'

They stared down the passageway, and about one hundred yards ahead of them there was a very bright light.

'Now that's magic,' whispered Wolfric.

'Come on,' urged Rosie. 'Let's get to him. I'd hate him to leave again if he thinks he's in the wrong place, and your torch is getting dimmer by the second.'

Taking to their heels they soon covered the distance between themselves and Oonie.

Skidding to a stop just in front of him Rosie said, 'Oh are we glad to see you Oonie. We thought we'd be stuck in this place forever. There doesn't seem to be an end to the passageway.'

'Hello Rosie, hello Wolfric.' greeted the unicorn unconcerned. 'That was an impressive whistle Rosie, I heard it without any trouble at all. I had a feeling you would need assistance soon when we first met. That is why I urged you to practice your whistle.'

'I'm so glad you did,' said Rosie.

'Do you know there are two shady individuals following you up the passageway?' said Oonie, looking behind them,

'No,' replied Rosie and Wolfric together, both looking around and feeling nervous.

'They must have come back,' said Wolfric. 'We saw them outside before we got stuck in this tunnel.'

'I think we should leave here as soon as possible. I for one don't relish meeting them,' said Oonie.

'Is it far?' asked Rosie.

'I think we will manage it, without too much bother. Wolfric here is a very fast runner when necessary, but I think you Rosie, will need some assistance,' said Oonie.

'What do you mean?' said Rosie, a frown on her face.

'How do you fancy a ride on a unicorn?' said Oonie.

'I would love to, but I'm no rider. We have a pony at Grandma Megan's but I haven't ridden for years.,' Rosie admitted.

'That's not a problem. Just hang on to my mane and I'll make sure you don't fall off. Wolfric, will you give Rosie a leg up please?'

'My pleasure,' he said.

Rosie stood on Oonie's left side, and took a couple of handfuls of his mane. She lifted her left leg and Wolfric cupped his hands so she could put her foot on them, and he raised her up enough so she could swing her right leg over the unicorn's back and end up sitting astride.

'We have no time to lose.' urged Oonie. 'Those characters are getting very close. Wolfric, although you will be running, hang on to my tail, and then we won't be separated. Ready?'

Wolfric just had time to grab handfuls of Oonie's tail, and before either of them could reply, the unicorn turned and sped off at lightning speed. All Rosie could see was a blur either side. She hoped Wolfric was alright behind them, but she didn't dare turn around to look.

It seemed like no time at all, and they were out in the open again, in a peaceful part of the forest. Slowing to a stop Rosie released her grip on Oonie's mane, threw her right leg over the unicorn's back, and slid smoothly to the ground. She turned to see if Wolfric was still with them. He was, although he was slumped on the ground still holding on to Oonie's tail.

'Are you alright Wolfric?' said Rosie, staring down at him.

'I will be as soon as I get my breath back,' he puffed. 'I thought I could run fast, but I swear that although I was using my legs, my feet didn't touch the ground.'

Rosie heard a chuckle from Oonie. 'They didn't my friend. I thought it better not to tell you and let you find out for yourself. I was a little worried you might refuse, and we didn't have any more time to lose.'

'Quite right,' agreed Wolfric.

Rosie went up to the unicorn's head and laid her forehead against his cheek. 'Thank you so much Oonie. I don't know what we would have done, or what would have happened to us, if you hadn't come to our rescue.'

'My pleasure,' he replied, his beautiful eyes sparkling. 'Remember I am always here to help you.'

Rosie nodded her head.

'Where are we,' asked Wolfric looking about him.

'We're not far from your home, but I would rather not go too near the village itself,' said Oonie. 'If you follow the path over there, it will bring you to the eastern entrance of Oakenveil.'

'Thank you,' they both chorused, turning to look in the direction Oonie had indicated.

Turning back to say their goodbyes, they were both surprised to see that he had silently vanished.

**

Back in the tunnel where Rosie and Wolfric had just been rescued from, the two unsavoury characters were left scratching their heads and wondering what had just happened.

The taller of the two said, 'I don't understand it, we were getting closer to them, I know we were.'

'I did see a very bright light in the distance,' said the podgy one.

'I saw it too, but how could they disappear like that? So very close and then gone. It would have been more to bargain with if we could have got hold of the girl as well.'

'What do we do now?' asked the podgy one.

'All we can do is return the way we came and keep watchful. If we're lucky we may get another chance shortly. But, we can't wait too long, time is getting short.'

Chapter 22

That same morning Jack, and Charlie, were at a loose end, wondering what to do for the day. They usually mooched about in the forest or sat around in their camp. Jack was particularly work shy, and Charlie just kept him company when he wasn't doing other things.

Jack's father was still drinking heavily to dull the pain in his broken leg, but this only made him extra bad tempered, and he always took it out on Jack. So, staying around the camp was out of the question for them, and they were dubious about going into the forest because of the frights they had had in there lately.

'I know,' said Jack. 'Let's take a trip to the duck pond beside Friston Church. It's not that far, and we have plenty of time on our hands. We can do a bit of fishing too, see what we can catch. I'll bring my small shrimp nets, and a couple of jam jars. We might even get some freshwater shrimp, a newt or two, maybe even a toad. You never know what's in that pond.'

'Alright,' agreed Charlie. 'I feel like a nice quiet day.'

They set off across the field, and were half way across when there was a loud explosion. They both dived for cover in the long grass, covering their heads with their hands.

'What the...?' Jack didn't finish the question because as he raised his head he was dumbstruck at seeing the warden, Fred Bennett, charging across the field in the distance, his shotgun held out in front of him.

'Look at that,' said Jack. 'We must be under attack of some sort. I've never seen that warden chap run so fast.'

'What should we do?' asked Charlie. He was trembling all over. All these frights of late were making him a nervous wreck, and he was never the bravest of souls.

'Let's wait a few minutes and see what happens,' suggested Jack.

'Fine by me,' agreed Charlie, sitting up and looking all around him. He plucked a blade of grass, and started nibbling the end of it hoping his nerves would soon settle.

After a short while, Jack suggested they carry on towards the pond. Nothing else seemed to be going on, and all was now quiet.

Just as they were nearing the edge of the large field there were two very loud whistles. Both boys again dived for cover, and Charlie had visions of tanks and troops emerging from the forest for the start of a battle of some sort.

Jack brought him back to reality by saying, 'This used to be a nice quiet place. I just don't understand what's going on. Come on let's run the rest of the way, it's not far.'

Staggering to his feet, Charlie raced after his mate and they headed off towards Friston church pond, anxious to get away.

After running for quite some distance they had to slow to a walk because both had a painful stitch. They decided to take a small detour to a nearby newsagents. They purchased a couple of bottles of lemonade, a sandwich to share, and some sweets to keep them going.

Arriving at the pond, they sat down on the grass and each drank half their lemonade. They were very thirsty after all that running.

'This is a lovely pond,' said Charlie, gazing at the water. It's crystal clear. I wonder how far down you can see if you look really close.'

They both felt a lot better after their drink and a short rest.

'We'll keep the sandwich for a bite later,' said Jack. 'We'll probably need something to help us on the journey home anyway.'

'Ok,' agreed Charlie, and standing up walked over to the edge of the pond. He started dipping his net into the water and dragging it along.

Jack walked a little further to the right, and did the same. For the first few attempts all they managed to capture in their nets was old pond weed, and a water boatman or two which they put back into the water. Jack then found a great pond snail, and happily stood with it in his hand examining it. He then half-filled his jam jar with pond water, and dropped the snail into it.

Charlie was getting excited because he had scooped up quite a few fresh water shrimps. They were on the small side, but he was delighted all the same, and transferred them from his net into his jam jar with water added.

There were some bull rushes around the sides of the pond, and some lily pads floated on the surface. A frog had been sitting on one of the lily pads watching them, and suddenly it gave a great leap, and splashed into the water.

'I'd love to catch a frog,' said Jack, as he disentangled a stickleback from his net and dropped it into his jar.

Charlie had managed to catch a couple of newts, and a leech. He was well ahead of Jack's catch, and felt quite proud of himself.

Deciding to have a short rest, Charlie lay down on his stomach and inched forward far enough over the edge so he could comfortably look down into the water without the front of his clothing getting wet. His face was only half an inch from the surface, and he was amazed at how busy it looked down there. All sorts of pond life swimming about, and different types of weed.

'Yikes,' he shouted, and his head snapped back so fast it's a wonder he didn't get whiplash.

'What's wrong with you?' asked Jack, only half concentrating on his mate. He was busy untangling something, he knew not what, from his net.

'Can't you smell it,' asked Charlie, pinching his nose with a couple of fingers.

'Smell what?' Jack stopped what he was doing, and sniffed the air. 'Now you come to mention it, I can smell something odd. Did you have eggs for breakfast?'

'No, I didn't,' Charlie retorted. 'It's coming up out of the pond, brown puffs of something.'

'See if you can see what's doing it,' suggested Jack. 'I haven't heard of anything in a pond doing that.'

Very gingerly Charlie lowered his face once again close to the surface of the water.

'Woah!' he cried, as his head snapped back for a second time. 'I saw a face looking at me,' whispered Charlie, fear showing on his face.

'What? Don't be daft. You mean a fish was looking at you or something.'

'No, a proper face, like yours and mine, except it was green. Everything was green, even the teeth. It was smiling at me,' said Charlie.

'I think you must be hallucitating,' laughed Jack.

'I think you mean hallucinating,' corrected Charlie. 'No, I wasn't, and I know what I saw,' he insisted.

'Have another look. I think you'll see your wrong,' said Jack.

'Not likely,' said Charlie. 'You have a look if you don't believe me.'

'Ok,' agreed Jack, determined to prove his mate wrong.

He placed his net and jar on the grass, and lay down on his stomach the same as Charlie. He was just about to inch forward and gaze down into the water when a green hand and arm emerged from the centre of the pond. A great eruption of bubbles also broke the surface.

'Aaahhh,' screamed both boys. They didn't hang around after that. Scrambling to their feet, they left the pond as quickly as they could, tripping and falling in their haste to start running before they were fully upright.

A loud peel of laughter followed them.

The water faery emerged from the water at the edge of the pond. She was very clever at camouflaging herself, and now transformed back to her usual self. She looked beautiful in the sunshine with her translucent skin and long dark hair shimmering with blues and greens. Very gently she picked up each jam jar in turn, and returned all that had been dragged from the water and trapped in the jars, back into the pond and the safety of their habitat.

'Nobody steals any of my friends if I can help it,' she said. 'Thanks to Mr Frog who alerted me to what was happening, you are all safe and back where you belong. Oooh look, they've left their sandwich behind. I do so enjoy a nice sandwich. Yum cheese. I haven't had cheese in a long time.'

Sitting down on the edge of the pond and dangling her feet in the water, she munched happily on the sandwich, remembering to drop some into the water so the others could also have a taste.

Chapter 23

Grandma Megan was getting quite worried. She hadn't heard anything from Rosie, or Wolfric, and wasn't sure what to do. She had decided to leave Mira out of the drawer where she normally kept her, because so much was going on, and she didn't want to miss any messages. Anyone who came to visit Grandma Megan wouldn't notice anything out of the ordinary, they would just think it was an ornate mirror. Also, if she did have an unexpected visitor and was concerned the mirror would call her, she just had to press a little button on the side and this would let anyone in Oakenveil know it wasn't a good time. Once the coast was clear she would press the button again, and the mirror was re-activated.

Just then Mira tinkled alerting her that someone in Oakenveil wanted to speak to her.

She rushed across the kitchen to the dresser where Mira was propped up, and Rowena was there smiling at her.

'Oh, Grandma Megan, don't look so worried. Rosie is fine. She is here with us as is Wolfric. They have had another adventure, but are safe and well. I'm sure Rosie will tell you all, once she is back home with you. She's having something to eat and drink now, and then Bertrum, will bring her safely back to you. I did suggest she could spend the night here with us, but she would rather come back to you.'

Grandma Megan dragged a nearby chair across to the dresser to sit down. She was so relieved her legs had gone a bit wobbly. 'Oh, thank goodness! I was imagining all sorts of things happening to them, when I didn't hear anything.'

'I expect you were my dear, but all is well, and she will be back with you shortly.'

'Thank you. I'm so glad you all insisted I have Mira. I don't know what we would have done lately if we didn't have her,' said Grandma Megan.

They made their farewells and Grandma Megan, gave a huge sigh of relief and sat for a while.

'What's up?' asked Trilby, who came flying in through the open kitchen door at that moment.

'Nothing's up, everything is fine, and Rosie will be back with us again shortly,' replied Grandma Megan, smiling at the little faery. Where's Cyan?'

'He's outside, talking to that weird goat.'

'If you mean Isiah, he's not weird, he was just born with one eye higher than the other. What do you mean talking to Isiah? Isiah doesn't bother with the niceties of talking ...'

Grandma Megan didn't bother finishing her sentence. Springing up from her chair, she ran to the kitchen door and scanned the garden. She could see a tussle between the two going on over on the far side.

Cyan had a vegetable pasty in one hand, and Isiah was trying to pull it away from him.

'No, it's mine,' shouted Cyan trying to keep hold of the pasty.

'Isiah, let go,' shouted Grandma Megan.

So, Isiah did just that, and Cyan fell with a bit of a thump onto his back, his little legs sticking up into the air. Isiah saw his chance, and picking up the little gnome by a trouser leg ran with him over to the manure heap, where Grandma Megan left all the poo and old straw after cleaning out the stables and the hen house.

'No!' shouted Grandma Megan running in their direction. But it was too late. Isiah dumped Cyan unceremoniously onto the heap, and in a mucky wet part too. In his surprise, the little gnome dropped his pasty, which is what Isiah was hoping he would do. The goat lost no time, daintily picked it up, and trotted off munching happily.

'You are a naughty goat,' scalded Grandma Megan, running towards Cyan. She stopped in front of the manure heap, and it was all she could do not to burst out laughing. She didn't want to hurt the little gnome's feelings, but he did look funny where he was, spread eagled and muck all over him.

'This stuff stinks,' grumbled Cyan, as he tried to get to his feet but only succeeded in slipping over and landing face down.

Luckily Isiah hadn't dropped the little gnome too high up on the heap, so Grandma Megan was able to reach across and grab the back of Cayan's shirt and lift him out. She didn't bother setting him down onto the ground, but said, 'Off for a bath with you I think my lad,' and marched off still holding Cyan upside down and a little away from her, glaring at the goat on her way back to the cottage. Isiah just stared back at her licking his lips.

'Oooh, honky,' chuckled Trilby pointing at Cyan. 'Are you going to have a nice bubble bath then?'

'What's a bubble bath?' Cyan managed to ask in between spitting out bits of poo and straw.

'You'll find out,' laughed Trilby, flying off to see what Erin was up to.

Carrying Cyan into the kitchen she placed a towel on the floor and stood the little gnome on it, instructing him to take off his clothes and put them in a pile beside him. She gave him another towel to wrap around himself whilst she busied herself getting his bath ready. Luckily Grandma Megan had a small tin bath in the shed, so this would be a lot better for Cyan to get in and out of, instead of trying to negotiate the large one upstairs in the bathroom.

Half filling the tin bath with hot and cold water, making sure the water wasn't too hot, she poured in a small amount of bath oil, and stirred it around with her hand.

'In you get,' she told the little gnome. 'Don't worry I won't look. There's a nice bar of soap there I made myself too, so make sure you give yourself a good wash to get rid of that smell. When you're ready, there's another towel to dry yourself. I'm going upstairs to fetch you some clean clothes. It's a good job I'm handy with a needle and thread isn't it. I just finished your new outfit last night.'

Cyan gingerly stepped into the tin bath. He wasn't too sure about this, but once he was in and sitting down he found it was quite enjoyable. He wasn't too sure about the smell of the bath oil, but thought it preferable to the smell of the gunk as he called it.

After washing himself all over, making sure all the soap was washed off, he carefully stepped out of the bath and towelled himself dry.

He was standing there wondering what he should do next when Grandma Megan came back downstairs, and presented him with a pile of clean clothes.

'Here you are dear. I hope they fit you alright. They're a lot smaller than our garments so they didn't take too long to make.'

Cyan accepted the little pile of clothes and dressed himself whilst Grandma Megan went to fetch him something to eat. This would cheer him up no end.

Walking back carrying a plate with some biscuits on it, she saw Cyan was standing twisting this way and that, trying to see what he looked like. Grandma Megan was pleased with the result, they fitted him perfectly. She placed the plate onto the table.

'Very smart, even if I do say so myself,' she said. Lifting down Mira, she held the mirror so that Cyan could see properly for himself.

'I like these,' said Cyan, fingering the garment. 'What are they called?'

'Dungarees,' answered Grandma Megan. Very serviceable for around the homestead, and it won't matter if they get a bit dusty or dirty. They're easily washed, and I have another pair half made for you. The shirt seems to fit nicely too. Now I've cleaned your boots and I've also made you another cap to wear.'

This cap wasn't like the one he had been wearing before, but a flat cap with a peak at the front.

'Thank you,' said Cyan, smiling up at her. 'These dun gees are very comfortable.'

'Dungarees,' corrected Grandma Megan.

'Ok,' he replied. 'Tell me, why do you keep all that gunk I was dumped in?

'That gunk, as you call it, is what I take out of the stables when I clean them each morning. I keep it because in time it breaks down and turns into lovely compost for the garden. All my herbs and flowers thrive on a feed of that every so often. It enriches the soil.'

'I see,' said Cyan. Grandma Megan could see his little brain ticking over and chuckled, but he didn't say anything further. Noticing the snack on the kitchen table he went across, climbed up onto the chair, and started tucking in.

'At least your appetite hasn't suffered,' she laughed. 'You stay there out of trouble while I go and ask Avery for his help to carry the tin bath outside to empty. It's rather heavy with water in it, and ungainly too.'

Cyan turned his head towards her and nodded. He was quite happy to do what she advised, and took another bite of biscuit.

'Ooohhh don't we look smart,' mocked Trilby, as she sat on the window ledge looking at him. 'Quite the little farmer.'

'Well I look smart, I don't know about you,' replied Cyan, looking in Trilby's direction.

'Now don't be cheeky, and don't speak with your mouth full. You're spitting crumbs all over the place, and it's very rude,' admonished Trilby.

He didn't bother replying further, just concentrated on eating.

Seeing that she was now being ignored, Trilby flew back outside to see what was happening out there. She had been to see Erin in the barn but he was busy dozing, stretched out in the straw, and didn't want to be disturbed as he was going to have a busy night ahead of him going out in the forest with Bertrum.

Grandma Megan, and Avery, had just finished emptying the water from the tin bath, and were drying it off ready to put back into the shed. Grandma Megan looked across and was delighted to see Rosie, and Bertrum, just entering the garden gate.

'Rosie, Bertrum,' she called, and ran to give her granddaughter a great big hug and shake Bertrum by the hand.

Bella had also heard Rosie's voice, and ran as fast as she could to greet her. Rosie scooped her up and Bella licked her all over her face. 'I think you missed me and were worried,' Rosie said to the little dog laughing.

'Oh, Rosie dear, am I glad you're safe and sound. I was so worried when the time went by, and I hadn't heard anything from you. Come along in both of you,' invited Grandma Megan.

'No, I won't come in, thank you Megan,' said Bertrum. 'I'll be getting back if you don't mind. The coast is clear so I'll take advantage of that.'

'I understand. Thank you so much for seeing Rosie back safely.'

'My pleasure,' said Bertrum. 'I'm sure Rosie here has much to tell you.'

Shaking Grandma Megan by the hand again, giving Bella a gentle stroke and raising a hand to Rosie. Bertrum turned, made his way out of the gate and with a quick salute to them both was gone in a flash.

'I wish I could vanish like that,' said Rosie, envy in her voice.

'I'm sure you will in the future dear. Study hard, and you'll be amazed at what you will be able to do I'm sure.'

Rosie grinned at her grandma and arm in arm they walked into the cottage.

Chapter 24

Rosie stopped dead in her tracks when she entered the kitchen and spotted Cyan sitting at the table dressed in his new clothes.

'Where's Cyan, what have you done with him,' said Rosie, pretending she didn't recognise him.

'Cyan looked across at Rosie and gave her a wicked grin.

'There you are,' she said. What happened to you?'

All he managed to get out before taking another mouthful of food was 'Gunk.'

Rosie turned to her grandma for an explanation.

'Isiah dumped him on the muck heap,' Grandma Megan explained. He was covered in it, so he had to have a bath. Luckily, I've been making him a fresh wardrobe, and you see the outcome before you.

'I think you look very smart,' complimented Rosie.

Cyan nodded his head in agreement.

'Now Rosie love, I hear you've been fed and watered, so to speak, so come, sit down and tell me all that happened.'

Rosie sat down at the table with Grandma Megan, and told her everything from the time she had left the cottage that morning.

'I'm so glad I've been practising my whistle,' said Rosie. 'We would probably still be stuck in that tunnel if I hadn't been able to summon Oonie.'

'I'm very thankful too my dear. Now tell me, who do you think was following you in the tunnel?'

'I really don't know, but Oonie didn't seem to like the look of them. It could have been those two weird characters we saw before we entered through the tree though. They must have come back and seen us.'

'Most odd. Now would you like some hot chocolate my dear? It will help you get a good night's sleep tonight.'

'Yes, I would please. I'll take it up to my room if that's alright. I want to consult Juniper and see if my crystal can show me anything more,'

'That's fine dear. You do what you want. I'm just thankful you're home safe and sound. But promise me you won't go out again or go flying tonight. Not too much studying either, you need your sleep.'

'I promise I won't Grandma. I think I've had enough excitement for today at least.'

'Good. You go on up then and I'll bring your hot chocolate to you when it's ready.'

'Thank you,' said Rosie, rising from her chair and heading for the stairs. Bella was trotting at her heels.

Reassured, Grandma Megan went to boil some milk to make Rosie's hot chocolate. She thought it best she carried the drink up to Rosie's room for her. Rosie was looking tired and she didn't want her to trip and spill any of the hot drink on herself.

A short time later Grandma Megan entered Rosie's bedroom carrying the hot chocolate. She stopped just inside the doorway. Rosie was fast asleep on her bed. Books were lying all around her, some opened, one or two on the floor, and she was holding her new crystal ball.

'Well I never,' muttered Grandma Megan.

'She just zonked,' came a little voice from the rocking chair.

'She what?'

'One minute she was checking something in a book, and the next she just fell back onto her pillows and was fast asleep. Zonked,' explained Trilby.

'Oh, I see. Well let me try to make her a bit more comfortable.' Grandma Megan went across to the bedside table and placed the cup of hot chocolate on it. 'She might wake up later and want something to drink, so I'll leave this here for her.'

Grandma Megan eased Rosie's shoes from her feet and put them in her wardrobe. Then picking up the books from the bed, she placed them in a pile beside the cup of hot chocolate. There was a blanket folded up on the back of the rocking chair so she collected this and shaking it out gently laid it over Rosie to keep her warm whilst she slept.

'Will you be here all night?' Grandma Megan whispered to Trilby.

'I will,' answered the little faery.

'That's good. Thank you. Bella are you staying here or coming back down with me?'

The little dog looked at the bed with Rosie fast asleep. Then she looked across at Trilby who nodded to her. Satisfied all was well, Bella walked across to where Grandma Megan was standing, and they both left the bedroom together.

Chapter 25

Trilby made herself comfortable on the windowsill sitting with her back to the wall and her legs stretched out in front of her. She watched as Grandma Megan gave Rupert a little more of the cough syrup, and rounded up the chickens making sure they were all in their little house safe and sound for the night.

Grandma Megan also made sure all the other animals were where they should be and had all they needed for the night.

A little later Trilby could hear the doors being locked and secured, and Grandma Megan coming up the stairs to get ready for bed herself. She obviously needed an early night herself, thought Trilby.

Keeping vigil at the window Trilby was wondering what was keeping him. Ah, good, there he was. Trilby stood up and put her face close to the glass.

Erin sauntered out of the barn, stretched and then turned to head off in the direction of the forest. He sensed someone watching him and turning around looked up at Rosie's bedroom window. He could see Trilby watching him. She waved to him and he bowed his head in return, then walked on.

That's good at least he hadn't forgotten, thought Trilby. She settled herself down again and was content to just sit looking out at the countryside. She would have loved to have gone with Erin, but knew she had an important job to do here, looking after Rosie.

Trilby didn't need a lot of sleep herself, and knew if she dozed off a little later, she would be wide awake in a second if Rosie awoke or got up out of bed.

Erin made his way through the forest until he came to the glade where the great old oak lived. He was a little early, so settled down to wait. He didn't have to find his own supper tonight because Grandma Megan had fed him before she had retired to bed herself.

He didn't have long to wait. Cornelius, the great old oak appeared in the glade, opened the small door and out stepped Bertrum, and Wolfric. They quickly scanned the surrounding area, then ran towards the trees where Erin stood waiting for them.

'Hello Erin,' greeted Bertrum. 'You know my son Wolfric, don't you? He insisted on coming with us.'

'Good evening to you both,' said Erin. 'Yes, I have met Wolfric before,' he said bowing to the young elf.

'Now, which way do we go?' enquired Bertrum.

Erin turned and led the way at a steady trot, Bertrum, and Wolfric, following close behind.

They soon arrived at the two large trees, and all three stood in front of them. Bertrum, and Wolfric, had both brought torches with them to use once they were inside. There was plenty of moonlight tonight so they could easily see if anyone else was about.

'Once we're inside, I think it advisable we keep as quiet as possible,' said Bertrum. 'No talking unless absolutely necessary. Keep your eyes and ears open. Now where is this lever you found?'

Wolfric shone his torch in front of him, and reaching forward found the lever easily enough. He clasped it tightly and pushed down hard. There was a quiet click and Wolfric opened the door, just enough for them all to sidle in.

Switching on their torches, Bertrum scanned all around making sure he located where the device was to re-open the door from the inside. They didn't want to become trapped inside.

'Here it is,' he whispered. That's good, quite easy to find. You can close the door now son.'

Wolfric did so, and they all started walking slowly ahead scanning the walls and floor. Erin didn't need the use of a torch; his eyesight was very good in the dark.

They had only gone about a hundred yards or so, when Erin stopped. He was slightly ahead of Wolfric, and Bertrum, and stopping so suddenly Wolfric almost fell over him, and only just stopped himself from uttering something aloud.

Bertrum looked at Erin enquiringly. The silver fox put his nose close to a certain part of the wall, looked at Bertrum, and then again at the wall.

Bertrum nodded his head and put his index finger to his lips. Listening intently, he was certain he could hear voices. He shone his torch up and around the area, and found a notch that ordinarily wouldn't be noticed twice, unless you were looking for it.

Wolfric could feel excitement mounting inside his stomach. Looking to his father for guidance, Bertrum held up three fingers. Wolfric nodded his head and got ready. Then Bertrum held up one finger, then two and on the third they burst through into a smallish room. Erin stayed by the opening baring his teeth to deter whomever was inside from trying to run out.

The two shady characters who had been spotted by Jack, and Charlie, earlier, and later by Rosie, and Wolfric, were each sitting on a chair drinking some sort of liquid from a bottle. They were so surprised by the entrance of Bertrum, and Wolfric, the taller of the two sprang to his feet, dropping his bottle, and knocking his chair over, whilst the podgy one fell over backwards still sitting in his chair, his legs sticking up in the air.

Bertrum and Wolfric lost no time using the surprise of their entrance to their advantage. Wolfric wasn't as tall as Bertrum, or as powerfully built, but he was very strong and headed for the podgy individual whilst his father tackled the taller of the two.

'Get em, Beaky,' yelled the taller one.

'I can't,' puffed Beaky. He's standing on my belly, and I can't move. Lance, help me, he's crushing my innards.'

Bertrum, silenced Lanky Lance with a punch to his jaw which knocked a couple of his teeth flying out of his mouth, but didn't knock him down completely. Bertrum, then followed with a quick punch to the stomach with his left fist, and another punch with his right fist which landed under the jaw causing Lanky Lance to bite his tongue, hard. He yelped and blood spurted out of his mouth. His eyes were watering, but he kept swinging his arms about hoping to somehow land Bertrum, a blow somewhere.

Erin was feeling a bit left out by this time, and decided to join in. He saw Wolfric had the podgy one pinned to the ground, and as he watched he saw Wolfric start to jump up and down on him. Beaky didn't have much wind left in him by now to try anything heroic.

Erin raced across the small space, launched himself and sank his teeth into Lanky Lance's upper left thigh.

'Aaahhh! Call him off, I give up,' begged Lanky Lance, as he crumpled to the floor clutching his leg.

Bertrum was very breathless with all the exertion, and was bending over Lanky Lance with his hands on his knees. He turned his head and said to his son, 'Are you alright? Not damaged at all?'

'I'm fine thanks. Didn't give me any trouble at all,' grinned Wolfric. 'Not what you might call brave souls are they?'

'Watch this one for me Erin. Don't let him move an inch,' Bertrum instructed the silver fox. He went across to the far corner of the room where there was a very frightened man, sitting gagged, blindfolded, and tightly bound to a chair.

Bertrum quietly spoke to him saying, 'I'm going to remove your blindfold so you can see what's going on,' and very quickly he untied the dirty old cloth that was wrapped around the man's eyes. 'Now for the tape over your mouth. I'm afraid the kindest way to do this is to rip it off in one swift movement,' and before he had finished speaking the tape was off.

'Hello, you must be Mr. Hepburn, Rosie's father,' said Bertrum to the frightened man.

Mr Hepburn nodded his head and was blinking his eyes furiously, trying to get used to the light.

'Let's untie you, and then we can use the rope to tie up these two.'

'Thank you. I remember you, you're from Oakenveil aren't you?' Rosie's father croaked. His throat was very dry, and he was very thirsty.

'That's right, my name is Bertrum, and this is my son Wolfric.'

Wolfric raised his hand, and smiled. He was having a great time still bouncing on Becky's belly.

'How did you find me?'

'It's a long story, but I think we'd better get you out of here and take you back to Oakenveil. It's closer than Grandma Megan's, and we don't want to frighten her in the middle of the night.'

Lanky Lance was still crumpled on the floor, not daring to move in case Erin took another chunk out of him.

Bertrum strode across to Lanky Lance tossing some of the rope to Wolfric on the way. Bertrum then unceremoniously tossed Lanky Lance onto his belly, brought his arms around behind his back, and tightly bound his wrists together. He then yanked him to his feet, but kept hold of the rope.

'Are you doing alright son? Want any help?'

'No, I'm doing fine thank you father.' Wolfric had stopped his bouncing, extricated Beaky from the chair, pulled him to his feet and was now tying beak's hands behind his back.

'Can you stand up and walk Mr. Hepburn?' said Bertrum. 'I realise you must be stiff in your joints from sitting in one position for a long time.'

Rosie's father slowly stood up and flexed his arms and legs. 'I'm a bit wobbly, but I'll be ok in a minute once the blood starts circulating again. Please call me James.'

'Alright James. I think the sooner we get out of here the better, just in case any more of them come. Wolfric, you go first with that scum, then if you would like to follow him James, I'll bring up the rear with this piece of baggage.'

They managed to get back out into the forest without too much bother. The two characters tried struggling hoping to break free, but it didn't get them anywhere.

Bertrum turned and closed the door firmly on the outside of the tree. 'I'll have to return later and make sure this isn't usable again, and repair any damage to the tree,' he said.

Erin decided to walk in the middle with James, and with the bright light of the moon they had no difficulty negotiating the forest.

'Hold on a minute Wolfric. I think the pathway is smooth from here on so it might be a good idea to blindfold these two. I'd rather they didn't see where we're going,' said Bertrum.

Wolfric yanked Beaky to a stop, and took the neckerchief from around his neck and tied it tightly around his prisoner's eyes. 'Can you see where you're going?' he asked.

'How can I with this thing on?'

'Good.'

Bertrum did the same with Lanky Lance, and they continued forward towards the open glade.

'Wolfric will you do the honours please,' Bertrum, asked his son.

'Pleasure,' said Wolfric.

Standing in the middle of the open glade Wolfric lifted his arm out in front of him and pointed his index finger with the magic ring on. He quietly spoke a few words in fae language and Cornelius slowly appeared.

Cornelius was just about to say something to them when Wolfric quickly signalled that he stayed quiet. He didn't want these two characters to get any indication of where they were being taken.

Cornelius silently opened the door and they all trooped inside. Bertrum gave the huge tree trunk a little pat before entering the door and looking up at Cornelius, gave him a wink. Cornelius winked in return and once Bertrum, and the rest of them were inside he silently closed the door and disappeared.

'Keep walking,' instructed Bertrum to Beaky, and Lanky Lance. Both seemed to be digging their heels in, refusing to walk any further.

'Where are you taking us,' demanded Lanky Lance.

'Never you mind, you'll find out soon enough,' replied Bertrum, giving Lanky Lance a good shove forward.

Continuing through the tunnel until they came to the little pathway, they crossed the little wooden bridge and were soon standing outside the home of Bertrum, and Wolfric.

Bertrum addressed James and said, 'Go straight in the door James. Wolfric, and I, will be with you shortly, when we've locked up these two.

James hadn't been in the elf village of Oakenveil before. He had heard a lot about it because he had married Grandma Megan's daughter Adele.

Walking through the door James heard a delightful tinkle of bells, and he was amazed at what he saw before him. From the outside, it just looked the size of any medium sized tree, but inside it was just like a large house.

Standing just inside the door, James wasn't too sure where to go or what he should do, but at that moment Rowena, appeared. She had been expecting Bertrum, and Wolfric, back, and was eager to hear how they had got on, but she was really surprised to see James standing alone just inside the door.

'James!'

'Hello Rowena. Bertrum told me to just come straight in. He'll be here himself shortly after he has made arrangements for the two thugs to be locked up' said James.

'Come in, come in, my dear. We'll go through into the kitchen and we can chat whilst I get you something to eat and drink. Then after you have eaten you can have a nice leisurely bath, and a good long sleep in a comfortable bed.'

'That sounds wonderful,' sighed James. 'But I must let Adele know I'm alive and well.'

'Don't you worry about that. We'll make arrangements straight away for her to be notified and brought here as soon as possible,' said Rowena.

'You are very kind, thank you. I must admit I am very hungry and thirsty. I apologise too for being so grubby, but they didn't supply the niceties of life for me.'

'Goodness, there's no need to apologise after what you've been through.'

Sitting down at the table, James watched as Rowena made a pot of tea and brought it across to the table. There were already cups, saucers, plates and cutlery laid out on the table ready for breakfast, so Rowena went to fetch a jug of milk and a bowl of sugar.

'Now you pour yourself out a nice hot cup of tea and I'll get your food. Nothing too heavy for tonight I think, your stomach needs to get used to being fed properly.

James poured himself a cup of tea and added milk and sugar. After only being given a small amount of water, if his jailers remembered, this tasted wonderful.

Rowena returned with slices of fresh bread that had been baked that afternoon, butter, various spreads, and a bowl of cereal.

'You tuck in to whatever you fancy. I'll join you and have a cup of tea,' said Rowena, and sat down in a chair opposite him. She had no intention of pestering him with a lot of questions. The poor man looked worn out, so they sat in companionable silence while James drank two cups of tea and enjoyed the fresh bread with butter and strawberry preserve spread on the top.

Rowena glanced across at James and noticed his eyelids were starting to droop.

'James,' she said quietly. I think it is time for you to go and take your bath. You'll sleep a lot better when you are nice and clean. Follow me and I'll show you where the bathroom and your bedroom is. Everything you need is in the bathroom and I'll get a pair of Bertrum's pyjamas, for you to wear.'

James followed Rowena up the stairs, trying to stifle his yawns as he went.

Rowena made sure James knew where everything was, and then went back downstairs to wait for her husband and son to come in.

She didn't have to wait long. 'Is everything alright?' she asked. 'Are either of you hurt?'

'No dear, we're both fine,' said Bertrum. Off to bed with you Wolfric, and thank you for your help. You did a great job.'

Wolfric grinned at his father, and headed off up to bed. He was feeling rather tired now all the excitement had died down.

'James isn't walking very well is he,' Rowena, said to Bertrum.

'Neither would I be, if I had been bound, gagged and blindfolded for goodness knows how long. Where is he?'

'He managed two cups of tea, something to eat, and should now be lying in a nice hot bath.'

'That should do him good anyway,' said Bertrum. 'Well, the two characters that were guarding him have been locked up for the night, and the elders will decide the best thing to do with them in the morning. Erin came back with us also, but he decided to stay outside under the stars.'

'Would you like anything to eat or drink before bed?'

'No, thank you. I'm beginning to feel a bit weary myself,' said Bertrum.

'Before you go to bed though, I would like you to check on James, just to make sure he hasn't fallen asleep in the bath,' said Rowena.

'I'll go and do that now,' he said, and climbed the stairs. Tapping on the bathroom door and not getting an answer, he opened the door and looked in. The bathroom was empty. He then went across to the spare bedroom and opening the door quietly peered in. James was tucked up in bed, fast asleep, and there was a gentle smile on his face.

Chapter 26

Grandma Megan was up bright and early the next morning as usual, and wondering how Bertrum had got on the night before. She had already fed the chickens and let them out to roam about, then fed the rest and put them out into their various pastures.

Noticing Erin wasn't in his usual place in the barn started her worrying. She hoped nothing had happened to him.

Mira tinkled on the dresser just as she was putting the kettle on the hob to boil the water for her morning cup of tea. Her heart flipped in her chest. 'I hope this is good news,' she mumbled to herself as she went across to see who was summoning her.

Bertrum was there smiling at her. 'Good morning Megan, what a beautiful morning,' he greeted.

'You sound very cheerful this morning,' replied Grandma Megan smiling at him.

'We all have every reason to be,' replied Bertrum. 'We have Rosie's father here. He is safe and well, albeit tired and very thin.'

Grandma Megan's hand flew to her mouth in her usual gesture when she was surprised or worried, and tears filled her eyes. She hung on to the dresser with her other hand.

Bertrum laughed and said, 'Once James has had his breakfast we'll bring him over to you. Someone has already been sent to London to inform Adele, and accompany her back to you.'

All Grandma Megan could do was nod her head, and wipe her eyes with her handkerchief.

'I'll let you get on now. We should be with you in about an hour or so.'

'Thank you, thank you,' was all Grandma Megan could manage.

'I expect you will hear all about it from James so goodbye for now,' and he disappeared from the mirror.

Grandma Megan blew her nose and raced out of the kitchen door running down to Avery's workshop, scattering the chickens in all directions as she did so. She had thought about letting Rosie know first, but then decided she would let her father surprise her himself when he arrived.

'Avery!' she called as she opened the top door of his workshop. This surprised Avery because Grandma Megan always knocked first, then waited for him to open the door, not wanting to intrude on whatever he was doing.

'Whatever's the matter Megan? You look in a bit of a state.'

'Avery, he's been found. James is at Bertrum's, and will be here in about an hour,' she managed to blurt out before bursting into tears again.

'Yes, yes, yes,' sang Avery as he did a little jig. He then noticed the state Megan was in, and went and gave her a big hug.

'Have you told Rosie yet?' he enquired, after releasing her.

Grandma Megan shook her head in denial. 'You know what she'll be like, charging off to Oakenveil which will be difficult for her because she won't be able to summon Cornelius. No, James will be here in about an hour, as I mentioned, he's having his breakfast with Bertrum and his family, then Bertrum will bring him here. I thought I'd go and wake Rosie and prepare breakfast, then she can see him as soon as he's walking across the field.'

'Good idea,' agreed Avery. 'This is wonderful news.'

Then Grandma Megan did a little jig of her own, turned and hurried back to the kitchen, again scattering the chickens in all directions. Avery laughed and re-entered his workshop.

'Well it's a good job this is nearly finished,' he chuckled, patting his latest project. 'Just in the nick of time I think,' he nodded.

Trilby was sitting on the windowsill, as she usually did in the mornings, and saw the exchange between Grandma Megan and Avery. She hugged her knees up to her chest tightly and gave a huge grin. 'Things must have turned out pretty well,' she muttered to herself.

Rosie turned and looked in Trilby's direction. 'Did you say something Trilby?'

'I think it's going to be a glorious day,' she replied, grinning at Rosie.

Grandma Megan went to the bottom of the stairs and called up to Rosie. 'Are you up yet Rosie love? I'm just starting breakfast. It'll be ready in about ten minutes.'

'Just coming Grandma,' she called back.

Rosie finished making her bed tidied away her nightdress and slippers, then went downstairs to the kitchen.

'Good morning Grandma. Trilby has just informed me she thinks it's going to be a glorious day. Hello to you too Bella,' said Rosie, and bent down to pat her little dog, who was sitting on her haunches, waving her little paws about, and smiling.

'Doesn't miss much that faery,' replied Grandma Megan. 'But I think she's right and it is going to be a glorious day. After breakfast, we'll just potter around the homestead, if that's alright with you Rosie love.'

'Fine by me,' agreed Rosie, accepting a plate of scrambled eggs on toast. 'It sounds like Rupert the rooster's throat is better now. I heard him waking everyone up earlier.'

'Yes, he's fine now, that syrup is good stuff, even if I do say so myself,' agreed Grandma Megan, sitting down to eat her own breakfast.

'Would you like some more toast Rosie love?'

'No, I'm full now thank you Grandma.'

Just then there was a sharp whistle from outside.

'Is someone else practising their whistling?' asked Rosie, relaxing in her chair.

Grandma Megan had a good idea Avery had been keeping an eye open, and was alerting her that they were on their way. She got up from the table and went to the kitchen door. She could see Bertrum, and Wolfric, with James, walking in-between the two. Out in front trotted Erin.

'Rosie dear, come here a minute.'

Puzzled, Rosie rose from the table, and joined her grandma at the door.

'Look at that,' said Grandma Megan, pointing to the field.

'Daaddd!' screamed Rosie, as she took to her heels and ran as fast as her legs would carry her to greet her father. She literally threw herself into his arms, and burst into tears clutching him as tight as she could. Bella wasn't going to be left out and was jumping up and down, barking her little head off.

One and all were a bit misty eyed, and Erin just sat down in the field and waited. Once they had composed themselves sufficiently, they carried on walking towards the cottage. Grandma Megan was waiting at the gate to greet them, and gave James a huge hug and a kiss on his cheek.

'Come in all of you.' she said, opening the gate wider and ushering them into the cottage.

Grandma Megan didn't know about anyone else, but she needed another strong cup of tea, and went across to fill the kettle and put it on the hob to boil. She then led the way into her sitting room where it would be more comfortable for them all.

'Sit yourselves down,' she instructed. Rosie not letting go of her father just yet, and waiting for him to sit himself down, perched herself on his lap.

'It was you I saw peering in at the window that night, wasn't it Rosie love?' he asked his daughter.

Rosie nodded her head.

Grandma Megan spoke for her and said, 'It certainly was, and if it wasn't for young Rosie here, none of us would have known anything about you being in this area.'

'Clever girl,' James praised, and gave his daughter a little squeeze.

'I see you're wearing your oak leaf ring again,' said Grandma Megan. 'Very clever of you to drop that on the dusty floor before they moved you. It was just the sign we needed to confirm you'd been there before being moved.'

'I knew Rosie would recognise it,' replied James. 'Bertrum returned it to me this morning.'

'Have you been hurt in any way,' asked Grandma Megan.

'No, I'm fine.'

'That's good, but I would like you to have a check-up all the same.'

'He's in a better condition than those two we captured last night,' laughed Wolfric. 'That tall one has a spectacular black eye and cuts and bruises all over his face, given to him by my father. Not to mention of course, the chunk taken out of his leg by Erin here.'

'You didn't do so badly yourself son,' said Bertrum, looking across at Wolfric. 'This young elf here, kept the podgy one occupied whilst I was dealing with the tall one, and spent his time bouncing up and down on the fellow's belly like it was a trampoline. Podgy has suffered three broken ribs, and a broken nose where Wolfric's boot caught him.'

'Did you really?' asked Rosie, impressed. 'Well done.'

The kettle must have boiled by now, so I'll just go and make a large pot of tea for us.

There was a tap on the back door and Grandma Megan went to answer it.

Adele was standing there looking very pale in the face, and her eyes were red from weeping.

Grandma Megan gathered her daughter into her arms and gave her a big hug.

'Is it really true,' Adele whispered in her mother's ear.

'It's really true my darling,' Grandma Megan, assured her daughter. 'Come,' she said, and taking her daughter by the hand led the way through to where James was sitting with the others.

James was in one of the armchairs facing the doorway, and saw his wife as soon as she came into view.

Rosie sprang up from her father's lap and flew to give her mother a hug. Her eyes were full of tears again, and she had another lump in her throat.

Adele smiled at her daughter when Rosie eventually released her.

Grandma Megan took Rosie by the hand and gently led her from the room, motioning to Bertrum, and Wolfric, to follow them out.

'But...' Rosie started to protest trying to turn around and go back into the sitting-room.

'No buts Rosie dear,' whispered Grandma Megan. Let's give your parents some privacy for a little while. You'll have plenty of time with them both shortly. They'll be staying here with us for a while,' and they all walked into the kitchen. Rosie went and sat down at the table.

'We'll be heading back to Oakenveil now,' said Bertrum.

'But won't you stay for a cup of tea, or a drink of something?'

'Thank you, but no, we'd better head back,' said Bertrum.

'Thank you both so much for all you've done,' said Grandma Megan. 'I dread to think what would have happened to James, if you hadn't rescued him. Where's Erin by the way?'

Bertrum, and Wolfric, walked out of the kitchen door. 'I can see him over by the barn. I think he's being grilled by Trilby. Is she behaving herself these days?' asked Bertrum.

Grandma Megan, and Rosie, followed them to the door. 'Oh yes, we haven't had any trouble with her. She's determined to help in any way she can, although sometimes it can raise eyebrows,' laughed Grandma Megan.

'Is that her handiwork I noticed in the kitchen?' asked Bertrum.

'Oh, you mean Cyan, the little gnome. Yes, that was Trilby's idea. She thought we could do with more help.'

'Mmmmm.'

'Father?' Wolfric, looked enquiringly at his father, then at Grandma Megan. Both had a good idea what Wolfric wanted, but waited for him to ask anyway.

'Yes son, what is it?'

'Could I stay here for the day with Rosie please?'

'You'd better ask Grandma Megan,' he replied.

Wolfric turned his head and looked at her, hope etched all over his face.

'I don't see why not,' she replied, smiling at the young elf.

'Thank you,' he replied, his expression changing to one of delight.

'Come along Rosie, time will pass quicker if you have something to occupy you,' said Wolfric, and they both walked down to the paddock.

'Grandma Megan watched them go, then she caught sight of a sudden movement out of the corner of her eye. Turning her head in that direction she saw Avery at his workshop door. 'I think Avery would like a word with you before you go,' she said to Bertrum. 'His arms are going in all directions.'

Bertrum bid farewell to Grandma Megan, and walked across to where Avery was standing waiting for him.

Chapter 27

Avery gripped Bertrum's hand and pumped his arm up and down. 'Congratulations, well done, what an outcome. Splendid! Now come along in and tell me all about it.'

Avery, and Bertrum, had known each other for many, many years, but nowadays they didn't see each other very often, because Avery now lived at Grandma Megan's.

Avery was quite content with this decision as it allowed him to carry on with his work undisturbed.

After Bertrum had relayed all that had happened the night before, Avery said, 'I have something here that you may be able to make use of. It's out the back, if you would like to see it. It's large, and I've had to extend the workshop to house it.'

'I'm intrigued,' admitted Bertrum.

'Come, follow me,' urged Avery, feeling excited.

They walked to the far end of the workshop, and went through a back door.

'If you'd like to stand there, I'll just take the covers off it.'

Bertrum watched as Avery walked across to a large covered object. With both hands, he clutched the sheets and yanked hard. The sheets fell to the ground landing in a heap.

Bertrum was speechless. He looked at the object, then at Avery, and then back at the object.

'What do you think?' enquired Avery.

'It's a rocket,' Bertrum managed to say. 'Are you serious?'

'Perfectly,' said Avery. 'We both know we deal with our criminals ourselves and don't involve the outside world. Somehow you must get those characters to the Court of Justice in Elmsville, and that's quite a journey. Anything could happen on the way, and it would be disastrous if they somehow got away before they arrived there.'

'But a rocket. Isn't that a bit extreme?' said Bertrum.

'No, I don't think so in the least,' said Avery. 'I've given this a lot of thought, and it has all sorts built in so it won't interfere with any aeroplanes flying about, or birds for that matter.'

'I can see you've been working very hard on this, but I can't give you an answer now. You must understand, I will have to take it up with the elders of the village, and then get back to you,' said Bertrum.

'Yes, I quite understand that. I still have a bit of work to do on it anyway, but if you do decide to use it, then it should be ready in about a week,' said Avery.

'Will there be room for two?'

'Oh yes, one above the other.'

'Well, I'll leave you to carry on with your work. It's been good seeing you again Avery. I'll send you a message via Mira, as soon as I know the answer.'

'Thank you, and it's been good seeing you again too. I really miss Oakenveil sometimes you know.'

Bertrum nodded his head, then turned and walked out of the workshop. Looking across towards the cottage he could see Grandma Megan, Rosie and Wolfric sitting on a garden bench chatting away happily. They spotted him leaving and waved. Bertrum raised his hand in farewell and made his way across the one-hundred-acre field towards the forest.

Whoomph!

Bertrum stopped in his tracks and turned to look back at the homestead. 'Avery!' he heard Grandma Megan shout. 'This will definitely need a lot of thought,' he muttered as he turned and carried on walking.

'Oh dear,' groaned Grandma Megan getting to her feet. 'Rupert's feinted again. Rosie love run and get the smelling salts for me. They're in the little drawer in the dresser.'

Grandma Megan crossed to where the little rooster was lying on the ground his legs in the air. She gently picked him up and carried him back to the bench. Rosie returned from the kitchen and handed Grandma Megan the smelling salts.

'Never a dull moment here is there?' stated Wolfric, looking around. The rest of the chickens and geese had made a dash for their respective houses and were still clambering over each other trying to be the first in. He stood laughing as he watched feet and feathers flying in all directions.

'My chickens will be featherless and nervous wrecks, if Avery doesn't stop doing that,' Grandma Megan grumbled. 'The rest of the animals are getting very jumpy too.'

'Is that why that goat has her head stuck under a bush, with her backside in the air?' enquired Wolfric.

'That's Janet. She's not as brave or as naughty as Isiah, and dives for the nearest cover,' said Grandma Megan.

Isiah was standing close to Janet with his head cocked on one side, obviously wondering what she was looking for and waiting to see what she would drag out of the bush. He got fed up with waiting for her, and gave her a push with his head trying to hurry her up. He caught poor Janet off balance, and she toppled further into the bush. All you could see was four feet sticking out of the top.

'Ooops!' said Wolfric trying not to burst out laughing.

'Wolfric, help Rosie get her out of that bush will you please dear? She's such a silly little goat, she'll probably stay there otherwise.'

Rosie got hold of two front legs and Wolfric clasped the two back legs and together they pulled Janet free of the bush. Once they let go Janet scrambled to her feet, shook herself and trotted off as if nothing had happened. Isiah quickly trotted after her wanting to see whether she had found something tasty under the bush and wanted his share.

Grandma Megan had finished tending to Rupert and bending down placed him back onto the ground where he strutted off, a little unsteadily, and again he had the hic-cups. Straightening up Grandma Megan heard peals of laughter. Turning she saw Rosie's parents standing hand in hand at the cottage door. Both were laughing fit to burst. That's good, thought Grandma Megan. Laughter is one of the best medicines you can get.

'Rosie, Wolfric, would you like to help me round up Hector please? I bet he's jumped the fence again and will be somewhere in the back field stuffing himself with the lush grass, which won't do him any good at all. He won't want to come back so it might be worth bringing a head collar and lead rope.'

'I'll get them,' offered Rosie, and she went into the barn to collect them from the hook beside Hector's stable.

'Good girl. We'll go on ahead and see which part of the field he's in.' Entering the field, they quickly scanned the area hoping the pony hadn't gone too far.

'There he is,' said Wolfric, pointing to the far side of the field.

'Right, you walk to the left and I'll go to the right,' said Grandma Megan. 'Once Rosie arrives she can walk straight towards him. Hopefully he's too busy enjoying himself and won't notice us creeping up on him.'

This wasn't to be. Hector although munching mouthfuls of the sweet grass was on the alert and saw them coming. Turning to face them he decided to go and meet them. He was within touching distance of Wolfric, when he swerved to the side and kicking his heels up into the air cantered in the opposite direction. Wolfric knew it wasn't worth chasing the pony, and followed him at a leisurely pace. Hector was a little disappointed that he wasn't being chased, and headed in Rosie's direction. Just as he was close enough for Rosie to reach up and put the head collar on him, he was off again, this time in a flat-out gallop.

Marissa, the little car had been happily dozing in the sun, but all the commotion had woken her up. She was parked in just the right position to see everything, and knowing this could go on for quite a while, she puckered up her grill and emitted an ear-piercing whistle. Hector's head shot in her direction, and before the others could move towards him, he cantered in her direction, cleared the fence without any difficulty, and went to stand in front of the little car.

'What do you think you are doing?' Marissa asked Hector.

'Just having a little fun,' he replied, grinning at her.

'Well I think that's enough for now, so be a good chap and just toddle off to your paddock.'

'I will if you tickle my nose first. You know how I like that.'

'Alright, but just for a minute or two and then I'm going back to sleep.'

Hector lowered his head down so his nose was just in line with Marissa's headlights. She had very long eyelashes and when she fluttered them they tickled Hector's nose and sometimes made him sneeze.

'Just one thing before I do this,' said Marissa. 'If you do feel a sneeze coming, please turn your head away from me. The last time you sneezed you splattered me with soggy grass and gunk.'

'Promise,' said Hector, and he strategically placed his nose in line with her eyelashes.

Hector was in seventh heaven for at least thirty seconds before he could feel a sneeze forming.

'Oooh,' he groaned.

'Quick go,' demanded Marissa, and reluctantly Hector turned and trotted away towards his paddock, sneezing twice on the way and with the effort of that also blasting forth with his rear end.

'Charming,' muttered Marissa as her eyelashes covered her headlights and she went back to sleep.

Grandma Megan, Rosie, and Wolfric, were now entering the gate from the field. 'Thank you, Marissa,' Grandma Megan, called across to the little car.

James and Adele were there to meet them. They had been watching all the antics and were feeling so much more relaxed and very happy.

'Is it always like this?' enquired James.

'Oh, never a dull moment my dear,' replied Grandma Megan. 'You haven't seen the half of it. Would anyone like a drink of something? I'm parched myself.'

They all agreed they would, and arm in arm they returned to the kitchen chattering and laughing as they went.

Wolfric would return to his village of Oakenveil in the evening.

Chapter 28

Jack, and Charlie, were sitting on the grass on the outskirts of their gypsy camp. Charlie was holding the silver cup in both hands, staring at it.

'So, what are you going to do with it?' enquired Jack.

'I've been thinking a lot about that,' replied Charlie. 'It's great I've found a piece of the treasure, but really, what use is it to me. I can't use it for anything, now can I?'

'So?'

'Well, if what you say is true, and it is proper silver, I might as well sell it and get myself something else.'

'Such as?'

'I've always wanted a bike, or some roller skates. Something like that,' said Charlie.

'Do you think you'll get enough for either of those?'

'Don't know 'til I take it somewhere and see how much it's worth. But I don't mind getting something second hand anyway. There's no way I would get anything like that otherwise.'

There was silence for a short while then Charlie said, 'Jack, if you come with me, make sure I'm not diddled, then I'll treat you as well.'

This was just what Jack was hoping his mate would say, and his brain started working overtime thinking what he could ask for.

'Where were you thinking of going then?' asked Jack.

'I thought I'd try Lewes. It's easier to get to than Brighton, or Eastbourne. What do you say?'

'What are we waiting for?' Jack replied, springing to his feet. 'Wait a bit, how are we going to get there?'

'Train from Berwick of course,' said Charlie.

Jack pulled out the inside of his trouser pockets. 'No money,' he grimaced.

'I have,' grinned Charlie. 'Well enough to get us there and back anyway.

'Where'd you get that?' asked Jack, amazed.

'Doing odd jobs here and there. While you're off setting your traps in the forest, I thought I'd see if I could get a bit of work at the village houses. I've been mowing lawns and doing odd jobs in gardens. It doesn't pay much, but it soon mounts up. I haven't told anyone else. Only me ma, and it helps her a little bit too.'

'Well I never, I didn't think you had it in you,' said Jack, surprised.

'Better than hanging around getting bored anyway.'

'Ok then, let's go. We can cut across the fields to the station.'

Arthur Zarik, had been keeping an eye on the two boys from a distance. He knew they were up to something, but didn't know what. He still wasn't very fast on his feet with his broken leg, and hampered by his crutches, so all he could do was stand and watch the boys head off across the fields. 'I'll tackle Jack this evening when he comes back,' he muttered to himself. 'I'll get to the bottom of what he's up to.'

Jack, and Charlie, set off at a trot and it didn't take them too long to reach the station. Charlie purchased their tickets and they didn't have to wait too long before a train arrived.

Climbing aboard they made themselves comfortable, and Charlie said to Jack,' Have you any idea where's the best place to take this?'

'I've only been to Lewes a few times, but I think there are one or two places that might be interested.

'That's good,' replied Charlie, and sat looking out of the window watching the houses and fields disappear as the train gathered speed.

In no time at all the train pulled into Lewes station. They headed in the direction of the exit and handed their tickets to the station master on the way out. 'Have you got the return tickets safe?' asked Jack.

'Yup, safe in me back pocket that has a button to keep it closed.'

'Good, don't feel like walking all the way back,' said Jack.

Walking out of the station they headed towards the high street. Lewes is a town with many hills and they were both out of breath by the time they reached the top.

'Which way?' asked Charlie.

'I'm not too sure, but if we just keep walking around and down the side streets, I'm sure I'll recognise one or two that my father used in the past.'

After a little while Charlie was starting to feel that Jack really hadn't got a clue where he was going.

'There's one,' piped up Jack, suddenly pointing across the lane to a dingy looking little shop.

Looking in the window Charlie wasn't convinced it was the sort of place he wanted to enter. It looked very dark in there, but Jack was already opening the door.

A bell jangled over the top of the door when it was pushed open, alerting the owner in the back.

Jack and Charlie stood in the centre of the shop looking around them.

'What can I do for you,' enquired a high-pitched voice. 'Buying or selling?'

'Selling,' confirmed Jack, before Charlie could open his mouth.

Looking in the direction of the voice, they saw a small little old man with half-moon glasses perched on the end of his nose. He didn't have much hair left on the top of his head but he made up for this with white whiskers all over his face. He had beady little black eyes and was wearing a grubby looking apron over a grey shirt, and black trousers. His shirt sleeves were rolled up to above his elbows, and his skin was very dark and wrinkled.

He looks like he could do with washing and ironing, Jack thought to himself.

'What is it then?' asked the little old man curiously. 'Show me.'

Charlie fished in his pocket, and brought out the little silver cup, placing it on the counter top.

The little old man looked at the cup, and then scrutinised the two boys.

'Where did you get this then?' he asked.

'Found it in the forest,' replied Charlie. 'It's not stolen if that what you think.'

'Which forest?'

'That doesn't matter,' snapped Jack. 'How much?'

Fixing a small magnifying glass onto his spectacles, the little old man reached out a wrinkled hand and picked up the cup. He held it close to the eyeglass, examining it in detail.

'I don't have much call for something like this,' he said, still examining the silver cup. 'More for watches or jewellery, that sort of thing.'

'I know it's solid silver,' said Jack. 'So, do you want it or not?'

The little old man placed the silver cup back onto the counter, and stood looking at the two boys. 'How much do you want for it?'

Jack said the first amount that popped into his head. Charlie looked at his mate in surprise, and the little old man threw back his head and cackled a crackly laugh.

'Come on Charlie, we're wasting our time here. I know someone who will want it, not far from here,' and Jack reached out, grabbed the silver cup from the counter top, and was just turning to walk out of the shop when the little old man squeaked.

'Wait. Wait a minute. I'm sure we can come to a compromise.'

'I'm listening,' said Jack.

'Ten pounds.'

'Keep going,' said Jack.

The shop keeper was starting to sweat a little. He didn't want to lose this. He had good contacts in London, and knew where he could sell it on with no questions asked, and make a very good profit.

'Twenty pounds.'

'Nope.'

'Let me see it again,' asked the little old man, and Jack handed the silver cup across to him.

'Thirty pounds, and that's my final offer.'

'Done,' agreed Jack, and smiled at Charlie who was standing with his mouth open. This seemed like a fortune to Charlie, never having had much in the past.

The shopkeeper went to a drawer under the counter, and counted out the money. Coming back, he went to hand the money across to Jack, but Jack motioned it should be handed over to Charlie. It was his silver cup after all.

Charlie accepted the notes, and folding them up placed them in a small pocket with a flap on front of his trousers. Should be safe in there he thought.

'Nice doing business with you,' said Jack, nodding to the shop keeper.

'Likewise,' agreed the little old man. 'If you find anything else in the future, I would be very interested.'

'I bet you would,' laughed Jack, and taking Charlie's left arm, they marched out of the shop, two very happy boys.

The little old man watched them go, and clutching the little silver cup in both hands, took it through to the back of the shop. A nice unexpected little earner, he thought to himself, and did a little jig.

Jack and Charlie had a wonderful time after that, going from shop to shop excitedly looking at everything for sale.

They were now heading back to the station, clutching their precious purchases and feeling very satisfied.

Charlie had treated his mate to a couple of boys' annuals that Jack chose himself. This surprised Charlie somewhat, because he didn't think Jack was much of a reader, but he did enjoy reading the adventure stories, and dreaming of being the hero himself. He also treated Jack to the sweets of his choice and a small aeroplane that Jack would have to build himself.

Charlie was very happy. He had purchased a second-hand bike that was reasonably cheap, and in good condition. This would help him get to his customers for the gardening jobs. He also had some sweets for himself and had treated his ma to a nice cream cake, and some toffees, and had money left over.

They had to travel in the luggage carriage on the return journey, because it was too difficult getting Charlie's bike in an ordinary carriage. But they didn't mind that, even though they had to sit on the floor all the way because there weren't any seats in the carriage.

They were both very happy sitting there eating some of their sweets, Charlie gazing at his new bike.

Charlie turned to Jack and said,' Do you realise this is the first time in a long while we've been out together, and haven't been frightened out of our wits by something or other.'

'You're right,' agreed Jack. 'Makes a nice change doesn't it.'

'Mmmmm.' agreed Charlie and giggled. He was so happy.

Chapter 29

A few days later Rosie was up bright and early. She had slept very well, and was thrilled both her parents were staying here with Grandma Megan, before returning to London in about a weeks' time.

Tip-toeing down stairs Rosie went into the dining room to her bookcase - cum desk, and lifted Juniper out of his secret hiding place. Carrying him back upstairs she sat cross legged on her bed and opened the old book of magic.

She hadn't done half the amount of studying she should have done, and needed to get to know how to use Juniper properly and how he would be able to help her in the future.

'You're up bright and early,' piped up Trilby, opening her eyes and stretching her limbs trying not to tumble off the rocking chair.

'Good morning to you Trilby, I hope you slept well.'

'I did, thank you,' replied the little faery. 'Are we having any adventures today?'

'I don't know about that, I need to buckle down and study,' answered Rosie.

'That's boring. I can tell you all you need to know,' said Trilby.

'I'm sure you will be a great help, but I need to get to know Juniper, and he needs to get to know me as well. The same applies to the little crystal ball.'

'Have you given it a name yet?'

'Yes, I have, but I don't know whether to tell you or not.'

'What is it then? I'll give you my honest opinion,' said Trilby.

'I'm sure you will,' laughed Rosie. 'Alright it's Selima.'

'Oooh clever,' replied Trilby. That means crystal in elvish. Very apt.'

'I thought so,' agreed Rosie.

'Go ahead then,' urged Trilby. 'Open up the book and get started.

'Wouldn't you like to go to the barn and annoy Erin?' enquired Rosie hoping Trilby would think it was a good idea, and leave her in peace.

'Not really, he's probably still out roaming around anyway.'

Rosie sighed and opened the book.

Inside the front were the names of many previous owners showing how many generations before her had owned the old book of magic. Rosie's name was the last one inscribed on the page.

Hello, Rosie Hepburn.

'Moby Dickens, you can talk!' exclaimed Rosie.

I can, replied the book.

'But why haven't you spoken before?'

I have, but because you didn't have the necklace on your mother gave you for your birthday, you couldn't hear me, Juniper replied.

'That's right, I haven't been wearing it lately. I put it on again last night when I dressed up for my parent's dinner party, to welcome my father home,' confirmed Rosie.

So, now you see why it's important you wear it all the time, said Juniper.

'It is such a beautiful necklace. I was a little worried about damaging it I suppose,' said Rosie.

You don't have to worry about that, advised the book of magic. *It is much stronger than it looks.*

'Alright, I promise to wear it all the time from now on.'

Good. I would hate you to miss anything I say. It might be important one day.

'Who are you talking to?' asked Trilby

'Juniper, of course. Can't you hear him?'

'I can only hear you,' said Trilby.

That's true, confirmed Juniper. *We are linking minds. That is why you must always wear your necklace, otherwise you won't hear me. Try asking me something by thinking of it and not speaking out loud.*

Rosie thought for a moment or two, and then asked the question by only thinking it. *Why don't you speak out loud?*

Because I belong to you and you alone. Do you remember Avery giving you a piece of paper on the day you found me in the bookcase? He instructed that you must never keep the two together.

Yes, replied Rosie.

Well, that piece of paper will instruct anyone who gets hold of me by foul means, how to communicate with me. That must never happen.

Why?

Because I am programmed to answer questions and help anyone who has the book if they can communicate with me. I hope you have that piece of paper safe.

Yes, it's very safe but why haven't I had to use it?

Because you are open to receive higher vibrations, unlike some, and you have the necklace. You can communicate with animals now, and soon your powers will strengthen.

'What's going on,' asked Trilby, watching Rosie closely. 'Why have you stopped talking?'

Rosie communicated with Juniper and asked him if it was alright to let Trilby in on the secret.

Yes, if she keeps it to herself.

'It's called telepathy Trilby, we are talking, but with our minds, not out loud.'

'That's not fair. I want to hear what's going on,' she complained.

'That's the way it works I'm afraid,' answered Rosie. 'Now I've told you, you must promise me that you will keep this knowledge to yourself. No one, and I mean no one, must know how I communicate with Juniper.'

'Seems a bit silly to me,'

'Well that's the way it's been for centuries. I think it's a good idea. Suppose somebody was watching and listening that shouldn't be. If they can't hear us, they won't have any idea what we're working on, will they?'

'I suppose that's true,' admitted Trilby.

'Now promise me,' insisted Rosie.

'Alright, I promise,'

'Good, thank you,' said Rosie.

'Rosie, breakfast is ready,' Grandma Megan called up the stairs.

'Oooh good, I'm so hungry,' admitted Trilby, and flew ahead down to the kitchen.

'Coming Grandma,' Rosie called back. Gently closing Juniper and lifting him up off the bed, Rosie ran down the stairs and headed for the dining-room first, placing Juniper in the secret hiding place. 'I'll speak with you tonight,' she whispered to the book as she closed and locked the little door.

Entering the kitchen, Rosie was surprised to see everyone already seated and tucking into their breakfast. Even Cyan was perched on his chair full of cushions at the end of the table munching on a piece of toast and jam. Trilby was sitting on the back of his chair dipping her finger into a thimble full of honey, and trying not to drip it everywhere.

Even Avery was seated at the table, which was very rare for him.

'Good morning everyone,' greeted Rosie, sitting down at her place at the table. 'It's a good thing Grandma Megan's got a large table, isn't it?'

One and all nodded their heads in reply, all having their mouths full munching on one thing or another.

A companionable silence reigned for a short while, and then Rosie's mother spoke to her daughter saying,' Rosie dear,

I think we should take a trip to London today. You need some new clothes, and we must kit you out in your uniform ready to start at the village school after the summer holidays. Your father is staying here to help Avery with something or other, they won't say what.'

'I hope there won't be any explosions,' said Grandma Megan, eyeing Avery.

'Not today anyway' he replied.

Just then there was a tap on the kitchen door. Grandma Megan rose from the table and went to answer it.

Rosie looked up in surprise, not because there had been a knock on the door, but that Grandma Megan hadn't been in a flap to hide Trilby, and Cyan. She must know who it is, thought Rosie.

'Look who's here,' said Grandma Megan, and she walked back to the table.

'Good morning everyone.' greeted Wolfric, as he followed Grandma Megan to the table.

'Moby Dickens,' spluttered Rosie. 'I wasn't expecting to see you today.'

'That was the general idea,' said Wolfric. 'We thought we'd surprise you.'

'Well it worked,' laughed Rosie. 'What are you doing here? What are you wearing?'

'Grandma Megan, your mother, and my father, thought it would be a good idea if I accompany you to London on your shopping trip. That way I get to see a bit of the outside world, so to speak.'

'Well you're certainly dressed for the occasion,' Rosie remarked eying Wolfric up and down.'

Wolfric was wearing a smart grey lightweight suit together with a white shirt, collar and tie. His feet were still encased in his black, soft leather lace-up boots. A touch of magic had been used to make his hair longer at the sides to cover his ears, and the green he liked to use as camouflage when out in the woods had disappeared.

Wolfric did a twirl. 'Feels a bit weird to me,' he admitted.

'You look very smart, my dear,' said Grandma Megan. 'We don't want people staring at you and making you feel uncomfortable, now do we? Rosie if you have finished your breakfast I think you ought to run upstairs and change into one of your pretty summer dresses for your outing.'

Rosie did as Grandma Megan suggested, and was soon back downstairs again changed and looking very smart and ready for a trip to the city.

'That's lovely,' smiled Grandma Megan. 'Now if you are ready Adele, I'll take you, Rosie, and Wolfric, to Berwick station. You should be in time to catch the London train.'

'This is so exciting,' said Wolfric. 'A ride in a car, a journey on a train, and I get to see the big city.'

They all climbed into Marissa, and were soon travelling down the country lanes towards the station.

A short time later Grandma Megan pulled into the station car park, and they all got out of the car. Adele had already bought the tickets, so they didn't have to worry about that.

'Now, you all have a wonderful time,' said Grandma Megan kissing her daughter, and grand-daughter, goodbye and shaking Wolfric by the hand. Then getting back into Marissa and leaning out of the open window she shouted to their retreating backs, 'I'll be waiting here to pick you all up at about six o'clock this evening. That should give you plenty of time to do your shopping.'

They all turned, waved, then carried on towards the station platform.

Grandma Megan started the little car and slowly pulled out of the car park making her way back to her cottage.

Chapter 30

Rosie, her mother, and Wolfric had a wonderful time in London going to all the large department stores. Wolfric had never seen anything like it in his life, and was amazed at the variety of merchandise and the crowds of people.

Rosie was kitted out in her new school uniform, which she wasn't too impressed with. She didn't like having to wear a uniform, but her mother also purchased various other items of clothing for her to wear after school and at the weekends, so this made up for it.

Wolfric was also treated to a new pair of long leather boots, and a waistcoat of many shades of green, which pleased him immensely.

After a busy morning shopping, they found a nice quiet café and went in to have something to eat and drink.

'So, what do you think of it all?' Adele, asked Wolfric, when they had finished their lunch and were sitting back relaxing for a while.

'I must admit to feeling a little dazed at the minute,' admitted Wolfric. 'So many people rushing here and there. Is it always this busy?'

'Most of the time,' answered Adele, laughing.

'I'll say one thing though,' said Wolfric. 'The food and drink doesn't taste half as good as Grandma Megan's.'

'I'll agree with you there, hers is very special,' said Adele, and Rosie nodded in agreement.

'Now if you're feeling up to it, I have one or two purchases of my own to make, and then we can think about heading home.'

Out in the street again, they walked towards a smaller store situated on the next corner.

Suddenly Rosie stopped in her tracks.

'What's the matter dear?' her mother asked.

'I have the strangest feeling. I must go this way, down this side street. Don't ask me why, I just know I have to.'

'Alright Rosie, love, you lead and we'll follow,' replied Adele.

The street had all manner of funny little old-fashioned shops, but Rosie was drawn to a little antique shop. It seemed to be stuffed full of every item you could think of.

'Can we go inside?' asked Rosie.

'I don't see why not,' replied Adele, and pushed open the door for them all to enter. A little bell on the top of the door jingled to let the proprietor know customers were entering the shop.

Once inside they weren't sure where to start looking first.

'Can I help you?' enquired a voice from the other end of the shop. A tall thin woman had just popped up from where she had been bending down underneath the counter. She was dressed all in black and her grey hair was coiled into a bun at the base of her neck. Her face and neck were extremely wrinkled, her nose was short and turned up at the end, and her mouth was very thin but wide. She wore a lot of beaded necklaces which jangled when she moved, and had many rings on her fingers.

'We'd like to have a look around, if that's alright,' replied Adele.

'Browse away. Just give me a shout if you want any help,' the woman replied.

Rosie and Wolfric headed off in one direction exploring the many tables containing all sorts of nick-knacks, games, and toys. There were so many different types of chairs, tables, wardrobes and other pieces of furniture which made it very difficult to squeeze in and out of to get to something that caught their eye.

Adele had found an old pestle and mortar which she thought Grandma Megan would love. This would make it so much easier for her to grind up her herbs and such she used to make her medicines and potions.

Managing to make her way to the counter to pay for the item, Adele was joined by Rosie, and Wolfric.

'Did you find anything you liked dears?' asked the old woman looking at Rosie, and Wolfric, in turn whilst wrapping up Adele's purchase and handing her back her change.

'Not yet,' replied Rosie. 'But I feel there is something here I need.'

'Well feel free to keep browsing,' replied the old woman, pleased that she had at least sold something.

Rosie closed her eyes and concentrated. She wished she knew what she was doing here. A picture suddenly popped into her head and she spun round pointing at a nearby shelf. Wolfric looked in that direction and said, 'I see it. Wait there Rosie, I'll go across and fetch it.'

Carefully he edged between furniture of all shapes and sizes. Reaching across he carefully lifted down the little silver cup with the oak leaves around the top and an acorn in the middle.

'Well I never,' breathed Rosie's mother. 'How did you know?'

'Magic,' whispered Rosie, grinning from ear to ear.

Wolfric passed the little silver cup to Adele who took it to the old woman. After much haggling with the proprietor, they came to an agreement and Adele paid for the silver cup and carefully placed the precious item into her handbag. She didn't want to risk losing it and that was the safest place she could think of. She smiled and winked at Rosie, whose eyes were sparkling.

Back outside the shop they were all so excited.

'I think we ought to be heading to Victoria station now to catch the train home, don't you?' said Adele. 'I can get the other things I need when I return to London later.'

Both Rosie, and Wolfric, wholeheartedly agreed. They were both starting to feel more than a little tired and were glad when Adele managed to hail a passing taxi to take them to the station in time to catch the next train back to Berwick.

Chapter 31

Grandma Megan was travelling back to the station in Marissa to wait for the London train. She wasn't sure which one her daughter, grand-daughter, and Wolfric, would be travelling back on but she was quite happy to wait, and had put her latest novel into her bag in case she had a long wait.

When she had left the cottage, James was fast asleep in a deck chair in the back garden. It had seemed a shame to wake him so she had gone to Avery's workshop to let Avery know she was leaving, and asked him to keep an eye on things whilst she was gone.

All was quiet at the homestead. The animals were either happily grazing or dozing in the hot summer sunshine, and the chickens and ducks were enjoying a splash around in the bath Grandma Megan had filled for them after lunch.

Avery was happily putting finishing touches to his project when he heard a commotion in the back garden. Walking to the open door of his workshop and looking out, he saw the chickens and ducks scattering in all directions squawking their heads off.

'What on earths got into them?' he muttered, scratching his head in puzzlement. He walked a little way out into the yard and heard a scuffling and a muffled shout. Turning his head in the direction of the voice, he couldn't believe his eyes. Two burley men with hoods over their faces were grappling with James. They had tipped him out of the deckchair and were struggling to march James towards the lane where an old battered truck was waiting, motor running, a driver sitting at the wheel.

'Hurry up,' the driver shouted. 'Someone's coming.'

'We're trying, but he's stronger than he looks and won't come quietly.'

'Of course, he won't you dumb dumbs. Bash him one. That should help.'

One of the hooded men stopped in mid stride, turned, and hit James hard on his chin.

James crumpled in a heap. Although he wasn't completely knocked out, his legs gave way under him which enabled them to drag him the rest of the distance to the waiting truck, and toss him in the back. The two then scrambled in the back after him. One pulled down a dirty old heavy sheet attached to the roof hiding them from view.

James was still only semi-conscious, so it wasn't difficult for one of them to bind his hands behind his back and stick tape over his mouth to keep him quiet.

'Stop!

Avery sprinted after them shouting, but he wasn't fast enough and by the time he reached the lane, the truck was heading off and gathering speed.

What was he to do?

An idea sprang to mind, and he turned and ran as fast as he could to Grandma Megan's shed. Flinging open the door he grabbed the nearest bicycle. Running with it he managed to throw one of his legs over the back, plonk down onto the saddle, find the peddles with both feet and start peddling as fast as he could down the lane after the truck. Unfortunately for Avery the bicycle he had grabbed was Rosie's and it wasn't very large. Avery being tall and thin, looked quite a picture speeding off down the lane hunched over the handlebars with his knees almost battering his chest as he peddled as fast as he could. He could see the truck up ahead and hoped his breath would hold out until he could either catch it up or at least see where is went.

Grandma Megan didn't have to wait too long at all for the London train to pull into Berwick and stop. From where she was parked she could see who was getting on and who was getting off the train, and spotted Adele, Rosie, and Wolfric, as soon as the carriage door opened and they climbed down onto the platform.

Grandma Megan walked quickly towards them. She was pleased they all looked very happy, although maybe a little weary, and they were carrying so many shopping bags between them.

'Well, you've obviously had a good time,' she laughed, as she met them at the gate to the platform. She took some of the bags off her daughter and Rosie, and carried them to the little car making it easier for them to carry the rest without dropping any.

Depositing most of the shopping in the back of Marissa they all climbed in and Grandma Megan started the little car. They chatted happily telling Grandma Megan all about their day, describing some of the things they had purchased and seen.

They were travelling down a very narrow country lane by this time and there was only room for one vehicle to use the lane at a time.

'What the…?'

Grandma Megan could see the old truck bearing down on them, and it was going much too fast. If she didn't do something, there was going to be a bad crash. Thinking quickly, she pushed her foot down on the accelerator and just managed to reach the very shallow pull in on their side of the lane, before the old truck shot past them.

'It's a good thing you're not too big Marissa,' said Grandma Megan, tapping the steering wheel. She was just about to pull out onto the lane and carry on, when Wolfric leaned forward from where he was sitting on the back seat and pointed ahead. 'Stop. What's that?' he asked.

They all sat staring ahead not quite believing their eyes.

Grandma Megan wound down her window and poked her head out. Avery was still peddling as fast as his legs, and the bicycle would allow, and as he sped past they all heard him shout, 'Can't stop. Fall off. James.'

They all turned around in their seats agog, and watched Avery as he raced down the lane after the truck.

Grandma Megan wasted no time in manoeuvring Marissa, and was halfway in turning the little car around when Wolfric said, 'Wait. Let me out. I can run faster than you can drive and I can pass Avery, catch up to that truck and stop it.'

'How are you going to stop it?' asked Rosie worried that he might be run over.

'I'm not sure yet, but I'll think of something,' he replied, as he quickly climbed out of the little car and sped off down the lane.

'Hang on tight,' instructed Grandma Megan, as she completed her three-point turn in five goes, and putting her foot flat down on the accelerator hoped she wouldn't meet anything coming towards her. She wasn't sure she would be able to stop in time.

Wolfric ran, passed Avery, and was now right behind the truck. He saw one of the men in the back peer out from the side of the curtain hanging down at the back. He knew he had to act quickly because they were nearing a junction, and this could lead to complications if any other vehicles were involved.

He jumped into the air and grabbed the knife he kept in his boot. Landing safely, he carefully took aim and threw the knife as far and as hard as he could.

Bang!

The knife hit the centre of the outside back tyre. It exploded sending the truck out of control, and the driver had no option but to brake hard and stop the truck, or land in the ditch running along the side of the lane.

Wolfric lost no time in jumping into the back of the truck, and grappled with the man nearest to him. He had the advantage to begin with because the men were still sprawled in the back after being thrown about when the tyre burst and the truck suddenly stopped.

Wolfric got a hold of the man's head and banged it hard on the floor of the truck knocking him senseless. The second one wasn't so brave and seeing that he was in for the same treatment held up his hands and didn't attempt to fight, but Wolfric punched him anyway to subdue him further, just in case the man had a brave moment, and decided to make a break for it.

Once the truck had stopped the driver flung open his door and attempted to run off, but Avery coming up fast from behind, ran into him with the bicycle and knocked him to the ground. Managing to steady himself and not end up sprawled on the ground himself, Avery threw himself onto the man and flung him over onto his back. He punched him hard in the face breaking the man's nose and splitting his lower lip. Avery was very glad this knocked any more fight out of the driver because he himself was exhausted from all that peddling, and he was sure he couldn't have endured a long tussle.

By this time, Grandma Megan had screeched to a halt. She sprang from the car together with Rosie and Adele. They all went running towards the truck to see if there was anything they could do, but all the fun seemed to be over and all that needed to be done was to rescue James.

Adele nimbly sprang into the back, knelt, untied James, then gently took the tape from his mouth. Tears were running down her face as she hugged him tightly.

'Are you alright? Have they hurt you anywhere?'

'My chin's a bit sore where one of them hit me, and a bit shaken up that this should have happened a second time, but otherwise I'm alright,' said James.

'Do you know why they keep trying? Have you heard them talking?'

'I don't know, but they are desperate to have me to bargain with. I do know these are just hired hands that do the bidding of someone else. Someone who wants to stay anonymous.'

They both got to their feet and Adele said, 'Let's get out of here. We can go and sit in Marissa.'

A few cars had stopped to see what was going on, and there was a small crowd gathered at the end of the lane.

Luckily a police car on its way back to police headquarters in Lewes, stopped to see what the fuss was about. Two police officers got out of the patrol car and walked towards Avery, and Grandma Megan.

They were told by Avery about the attempted kidnapping, and how he had chased them on the bicycle. And how Grandma Megan, who was returning home from the station with her daughter, grand-daughter and friend, saw what was happening and joined in the chase. Avery decided not to mention Wolfric's race to catch up with the truck and puncturing the lorry tyre by throwing his knife. They would ask too many questions, and he didn't want Wolfric to be taken away in the police car.

The kidnappers were still looking very groggy, but the police officers decided not to take any chances and radioed to Lewes for reinforcements together with a police van to transport the villains back to the station. This didn't take long to arrive and the villains were loaded into the van. One of the police constables from the patrol car went with them and the other stayed behind.

Grandma Megan, and the rest of her family could go back to the homestead where police officers would call later to take statements. They had been through enough for now, and shock was starting to set in with all of them.

Adele was already seated in the back seat of Marissa with James, so Rosie climbed into the passenger seat, and Grandma Megan into the driver's seat.

'Well, I think it's a good job the police are going to deal with those three. Bertrum has enough to deal with deciding what to do with the two he already has at Oakenveil,' said Grandma Megan, quietly.

The police officer offered Avery, and Wolfric, a lift back to the cottage, seeing that the little car was full, and he also put the bicycle into the boot of the police car. The poor bicycle was rather buckled and would need some attention before it could be ridden again, but Avery was very much up to the job.

Marissa lead the way back to Grandma Megan's cottage with the patrol car following.

Wolfric was thrilled to be having a ride in a police car. What a day he'd had. A trip to London, train rides, shopping in large department stores, and a kidnapping rescue. He couldn't help the big grin on his face. He was sitting in the back of the patrol car and Avery was in the passenger seat in front next to the driver. The police officer glanced in his rear-view mirror and saw the big grin on the boy's face. He thought it was from joy and excitement. All boys wanted to have a ride in a police car, and he was happy to oblige.

Wolfric was thrilled and excited to be travelling in a police car. He would have a lot to tell his parents. But the big grin on his face was because he was wondering what the constable would say if he knew he had two wood elves as passengers.

Chapter 32

Trilby was sitting up in a tree near the homestead watching and waiting for Grandma Megan to return. How was she going to tell her that James had been kidnapped again! She had heard the commotion in the garden that afternoon and flown to Rosie's bedroom window in time to see the men drag James away, and Avery giving chase on Rosie's bicycle. He really should have picked one of the larger bicycles, she thought. Hoping she wasn't going to be in trouble for not giving chase herself, when she had told Erin what had happened he'd advised her to stay put and to keep an eye on the place because everyone else had gone out and only the animals remained. It wasn't good for the homestead to be left unattended.

Seeing something out of the corner of her eye, she turned her head and was relieved to see Marissa slowly crossing the little bridge and heading home. The police patrol car following behind alarmed her, and she sprang into action flying off to make sure Cyan, and Erin, were out of sight until it had gone.

Marissa came to a stop outside the back gate, and the patrol car drew up close behind. Trilby was astonished when she saw Grandma Megan, Rosie, Adele and James get out of the little car, but she was really staggered when she saw Avery, and Wolfric, get out of the patrol car.

The police constable shook hands with them all, confirmed someone would be back to take their statements, probably tomorrow. He lifted the bicycle out of the boot of the patrol car and handed it to Avery, touched his cap in a salute, got back into his car and drove off.

Trilby watched him go from her hiding place before she flew down and into the kitchen where Grandma Megan was putting the kettle on to boil to make tea for the grownups and hot drinks for Rosie and Wolfric. The shopping had been carried in. There seemed to be bags all over the place.

Bella was so excited to see Rosie back home again, and after bouncing around, greeting everyone and having a quick cuddle from Rosie, she went across to investigate all the bags on the floor. Sticking her little nose in each one in turn, she was hoping there would be something in one of them for her. Rosie laughed at the little dog's antics. Bella was now sitting beside one of the bags, her little paws waving about in the air.

'You've found it haven't you. What a clever girl you are,' praised Rosie, and bending down she reached into the bottom of the carrier bag and produced a packet of meaty chews that Bella was very partial to. Unwrapping the packet, Rosie took one out and gave it to the little dog. Bella took the treat very gently and carried it off to her basket to enjoy.

Trilby went to the door of the sitting-room, opened it and beckoned Cyan to come out.

Grandma Megan noticed and said, 'Oh thank you Trilby, what a clever little faery you are. I hadn't thought about explaining that away.'

'You're welcome,' said Trilby, pleased to know she had done the right thing. 'I'll just go and let Erin know the coast is clear also.'

Grandma Megan nodded to Trilby, and carried on making the hot drinks. Best thing for shock she thought, even though everyone seemed to be rallying around quickly.

Sitting at the table a short time later, Rosie was enjoying showing her grandma all her new clothes. She also had a gift of stemmed ginger for Grandma Megan, and treacle toffee for her Uncle Avery.

Wolfric was also thrilled with his new boots and waistcoat, and put them on to show Grandma Megan.

Trilby was feeling a little left out by now until Rosie walked across to where the little faery was sitting on a shelf on the kitchen dresser. Rosie handed her a small box.

'For me?' asked Trilby, surprised.

'Of course, for you. You don't think I would forget you, do you?'

Trilby opened the little box and neatly folded inside was a red and blue check shirt together with a blue pair of dungarees, like the ones made for Cyan.

Trilby unfolded both items and held them up for all to see.

Grandma Megan looked at Rosie with a puzzled expression on her face.

Rosie laughed at her, and explained. 'Our Trilby here is always up trees or around the garden, and I thought if she had something like these to wear, then it wouldn't matter if she got them dirty or torn, and she wouldn't be ruining her beautiful dress.'

'You're a clever girl, and very thoughtful,' praised Grandma Megan.

Trilby flew off with both items to change in private.

'Where on earth did you find them?' asked Grandma Megan.

'Well they're doll's clothes really, but I'm not going to tell Trilby that. I'm sure she doesn't want to be reminded about being a doll,' said Rosie. 'I thought they would be more serviceable, and warmer for her as she isn't protected by the veil in Oakenveil now. I'll have to get her a coat or jacket a bit later too, ready for the winter.'

Grandma Megan gave Rosie a big hug, and they all admired Trilby in her new outfit when she reappeared back in the kitchen.

'They are very comfortable,' said Trilby, as she gave a twirl in mid-air.

'Now who looks like a farm girl,' piped up Cyan, getting his own back on Trilby for making fun of him when he had his new dungarees on.

Trilby wasn't at all upset, but stuck her tongue out at him none the less, and gave another twirl.

'We have something for you too,' said Adele, handing her mother her package,

'Really? You didn't need to you know,' said Grandma Megan, accepting the package.

Unwrapping her gift, Grandma Megan was thrilled and said, 'This is just what I need. My old one is almost worn out, I've used it so much. It isn't as sturdy as this nice new one. Thank you.'

Avery wasn't left out either. They had got him a new cravat in cherry red. He loved wearing cravats.

'Did you get anything for yourself?' Grandma Megan, asked her daughter.

'I have my James back. That is all I need,' she replied, smiling across the table at her husband. 'Oh, I nearly forgot,' she continued reaching across for her handbag. Opening it, she took out the small package and handed it to Grandma Megan.

'What's this? Another one?'

Unwrapping the small package and holding the little silver cup in her hands, Grandma Megan couldn't help herself and getting up from her seat did a little jig around the kitchen holding the little silver cup aloft.

'Yes, yes, yes,' she sang. 'Where on earth did you find it? I've been really worried we wouldn't see it again, and Cornelius has been getting weaker and weaker.'

Rosie, Adele, and Wolfric, each contributed to the story of how they had found the little silver cup.

'I'm so relieved,' breathed Grandma Megan, sitting down again at the table. 'Cornelius must have the elixir on the night of the next new moon, which is very soon. Any later and it might be too late for him to recover sufficiently.'

Wolfric decided it was now time for him to return home to Oakenveil. He thanked Adele for her generosity, and for giving him such a day to remember.

'You are very welcome. It's the least I could do after the brave rescue you and your father accomplished,' replied Adele. 'And, your help in rescuing James today. I will always be in your debt.'

'Nonsense,' replied Wolfric. 'I do like a good adventure, as I've said before.'

'Oh, before you go, I still have the sweets I bought for you at the county fair,' said Rosie, going to collect them.

Returning quickly, she handed Wolfric the paper bag. 'They're called flying saucers. I hope you like them.'

Wolfric accepted the gift and thanked Rosie for her thoughtfulness. He opened the bag and looked inside. They did indeed look like miniature flying saucers, and were all different colours.

He couldn't resist trying one. They didn't have anything like this in Oakenveil. Popping one into his mouth he was rather surprised to find it stuck to the roof of his mouth and on sucking it harder to try and dislodge it, all the sherbet inside the sweet exploded into his mouth. He had a coughing fit and his eyes were streaming.

Rosie was mortified. She had forgotten to tell him the best way she had found to eat them was to nibble a little of the wafer on the outside to make a hole, and then tip the sherbet into the mouth and let it dissolve slowly, then eat the rest.

After Wolfric had managed to compose himself and dry his eyes, she did explain this to him.

'I'll remember for the next time,' he promised.

Wolfric then said his goodbyes to the rest of the family. Grandma Megan, and Rosie accompanied him to the gate and watched him head off across the one-hundred-acre field towards home, carrying his parcels.

These flying saucers will be a great trick to play on some of the young elves tomorrow, he thought, as he made his way back to Cornelius. He was chuckling to himself as he walked along.

Grandma Megan linked arms with Rosie, and they turned and walked back into the cottage.

'Hungry?' asked Grandma Megan.

'Starving,' replied Rosie laughing.

Grandma Megan stood for a moment looking around the room. After such a long time living in her cottage with only Avery and her animals for company, it was so nice to have her family around her again. She knew Adele, and James, would be returning to London very soon, but she was sure they would visit frequently, now that Rosie would be living here with her.

She also included Trilby, and Cyan, as part of her family now, and wouldn't have had it any other way.

Chapter 33

Bertrum had been very busy lately having all sorts of meeting with the elders concerning the two villains that had kidnapped James. They all agreed there was no doubt that Lanky Lance, and Beaky, were guilty, but the elders all had varying opinions concerning the best way to transport them to the secure prison hundreds of miles away, and to thwart any rescue attempts made along the way.

The decision was obvious really, once Wolfric had arrived back home a few days earlier from his outing to London and told them about the second kidnapping attempt on James, and how he had been rescued again.

'Well, I think we'll have to take Avery up on his offer and use the rocket,' said Bertrum. 'I'm a bit dubious about doing so, but I don't see any alternative.'

'Avery is a good inventor,' said Fitz, one of the elders who believed in Avery. 'His inventions sometimes go a little awry during the process, but in the end, he masters what he is aiming for, and leaves nothing to chance.'

'I agree,' said Bertrum, and the others had no option but to approve the decision. 'I'll contact Avery, via Mira, to let him know, and I'll find out when it will be ready to use. Once we know that, then we can transport the prisoners to him one night.'

They all nodded their approval, and Bertrum went back to his home to call up Avery. He would be happy once those two were well away from Oakenveil, and James and his family.

Grandma Megan was in the kitchen as usual busy preparing more creams and potions from her herbs. She used these daily now, for one thing or another.

Mira tinkled her merry tune on the dresser letting her know someone from Oakenveil was waiting to speak with her.

Wiping her hands on her apron she went across and was surprised to see Bertrum smiling at her.

'Hello Bertrum, how is everything with you this bright sunny day?'

'Hello, to you also Megan,' Bertrum replied. 'Everything is just fine. I'm sorry to bother you, I can see that you're busy, but could I have a quick word with Avery please?'

'Of course, you can. I'll just get him for you.'

Grandma Megan made her way down to Avery's workshop calling his name as she went.

'Avery, Avery.'

'What's the matter? Is something wrong?' asked Avery, coming to his workshop door.

'I don't think so, but Bertrum is wanting a word with you via Mira. He's waiting for you.'

Avery sprinted up to the cottage. Grandma Megan watched him go and thought he really was very agile, considering his considerable age.

Walking back into her kitchen, Grandma Megan was just in time to hear the part of the conversation where a rocket was mentioned.

'Rocket!' she screeched.

Avery turned his head and put his right index finger to his lips for her to be silent so he could finish his conversation with Bertrum.

'Oh my,' muttered Grandma Megan, sitting down on one of the kitchen chairs.

Avery finished speaking with Bertrum saying he would be in touch in a couple of days. It shouldn't take too much longer to iron out the kinks.

Guessing he was now in for a grilling by Grandma Megan, Avery quickly turned and headed for the kitchen door saying as he went, 'Must rush, lots to do now.'

'Avery, you come back here and tell me what's going on,' shouted Grandma Megan, rising from her chair and rushing after him.

'What's going on?' said Rosie, to Cyan. They were both checking her little garden, and stood watching Grandma Megan chasing Avery down to his workshop. 'It must be serious. Grandma Megan doesn't usually chase after Avery shouting like that.'

Cyan didn't bother trying to answer because he was busy munching on a fruit scone.

Rosie looked down at the little gnome and said, 'You know, I think you ought to try and stop eating so much. Try and wait for meal times.'

Cyan just grinned at her, and took another bite of his scone.

Grandma Megan followed Avery into his workshop, not bothering to wait and be invited this time.

'Avery, come here and explain what's going on,' she demanded.

Avery now knew it wasn't any good trying to hide the plan from Grandma Megan any longer. He stopped walking, gave a huge sigh, and turned to face her.

'Now, try and keep calm Megan,' he said. 'I'll take you out the back of the workshop and show you, if you promise to think this through rationally.'

Grandma Megan nodded her head, and Avery beckoned her to follow him.

Opening the door at the back of his workshop he walked through holding up his hand for Grandma Megan to stand where she was.

He crossed to where the rocket was standing covered by sheets. Reaching up he pulled down one sheet after the other and revealed the bright red rocket in all its glory.

All Grandma Megan could do was stand there with her mouth open, her eyes were enormous. She glanced at Avery and then back at the rocket.

Avery saw this was rather a shock for her, and walked back to where she was standing.

'Come with me and I'll explain,' he said, taking her by her right arm and leading her back through the workshop, up the stairs to his living quarters, and across to one of his armchairs, where Grandma Megan sat down with a plop.

'I'm sure you have a lot of questions,' said Avery.

Grandma Megan nodded her head, but she was still speechless.

'Let me try and explain,' said Avery. 'I've always dreamt of building a rocket, but it was impossible all the time I was living in Oakenveil. Much too dangerous with the precious veil concealing the village. If that was damaged it would be disastrous as you know.'

Grandma Megan just sat staring at him.

'Well anyway, the elders were getting a little itchy with some of my inventions, so that was when it was suggested I come here to live with you. I was delighted with the arrangement as you know, and you generously allowed me to use this building and left me alone to do what I wanted.'

He paused and looked at Grandma Megan, but she just sat there with her eyes glued to his face not saying a word.

Avery continued. 'Don't you see Megan, it was just too good an opportunity for me, and I only meant to build a small rocket, but it grew and grew until it ended up the size you saw a few minutes ago. Then I got to thinking. Those villains that were holding James need to be transported to the jail at Elmsville without any attempts to break them free. There's no doubt they are guilty, because Bertrum, and Wolfric, caught them red handed, overpowered them and rescued James. When Bertrum was here the other day I showed him the rocket and he was going to speak with the other elders and get back to me to let me know if they thought the idea was viable. They are all in full agreement now, since the second attempt to kidnap James, and Bertrum, wants to know when it will be ready to use.'

'You'll blow us all up,' Grandma Megan, whispered.

'No, no. It's very safe, really. I've built it so I can control it from here, and it won't interfere with any aircraft, birds or anything else flying about.'

'When and where will this take place?' asked Grandma Megan.

'I can have it ready in four days' time. We'll use one of the far fields so we have privacy. It'll take place late at night and the elders will deliver the villains straight to the rocket, so they won't have to come anywhere near here.'

'Are you sure it's as safe as you say it is?'

'I'm sure. I wouldn't do anything to put you, your homestead, or family in any danger. You should know that Megan.'

Grandma Megan nodded her head. 'I have always trusted you Avery. I think it's the surprise. That was the last thing I expected to see.'

Avery sat and grinned at her, then a huge smile appeared on Grandma Megan's face. 'Those villains will get a bit of a shock, won't they? I bet they think they'll be able to escape on the journey to Elmsville.'

They both then sat and laughed, until the tears flowed down their cheeks.

Chapter 34

Grandma Megan was sitting at the kitchen table surrounded by cleaning cloths and polish. She was holding the little silver cup in one hand busy buffing it with a soft cloth held in her other hand. It had looked rather the worse for wear after all it had been through lately, but now it was bright and shiny again. Satisfied she had done all she could, she carried the little cup across to the dresser and placed it in a little cupboard near the top, loath to leave it out in full view in case it went missing again. That would be disastrous. Tonight, there would be a new moon and Cornelius must be given the elixir of life from it, to save both his life, and that of Oakenveil. Walking back to the table she cleared away all the cloths and polish, then washed down the table. Everyone would be getting up soon and it was time to get the breakfast ready.

Happily humming to herself she filled the kettle with water and put it on the stove to boil. A nice cup of tea would go down well now, she thought to herself.

She had fed Bella and Amber earlier, and they were both outside enjoying the early morning. Bella kept watch making sure Amber didn't get into any trouble. The little kitten was growing up fast, but Bella still took her duties of looking after her very seriously.

Cyan was now waking up in his little bed in the large kitchen. Sitting up, stretching and yawning he looked about him.

'Good morning Cyan,' greeted Grandma Megan. 'I hope you slept well.'

'I did, thank you,' he replied, turning and smiling at her.

'That's good. Breakfast will be ready once you have washed and changed out of your pyjamas.'

Bowing to her Cyan then collected his clothes from the little chair nearby and walked off into the next room where Grandma Megan had organised his own little bathroom, with a touch of magic of course.

She could now hear the others moving around upstairs getting ready for the day. It had been a very special time for her lately, with her daughter, grand-daughter and James staying here.

In a couple of days, Adele and James would be returning to London, but she was sure they wouldn't leave it too long between visits.

Adele, Rosie, and James, all came downstairs and arrived in the kitchen together.

'Where's Avery,' enquired James, as they seated themselves at the table. He liked Avery, and was very interested in his inventions.

'He's putting the finishing touches to the rocket,' answered Grandma Megan. 'I do hope he knows what he's doing. I must admit I'm a little worried.'

Cyan had come back into the kitchen now, dressed and ready for the day. He walked across to the table, and Grandma Megan bent down and lifted him into his chair. Cyan didn't waste any time and reached out to his plate for a piece of toast and jam.

'Everything will be fine, you'll see,' said Adele, trying to reassure her mother.

Whoomph!

Everyone at the table jumped in surprise, and Cyan fell off his chair and landed in a heap under the table.

'You were saying dear?' enquired Grandma Megan, looking at her daughter as she rose from the table. She bent down picked up the little gnome and sat him back in his chair. His piece of toast and jam was now stuck to his forehead. Grandma Megan peeled it off and placed it back onto his plate before hurrying off to fetch a flannel and towel to wash his face. Cyan didn't mind there wasn't as much jam left on the toast, he picked it up and happily started eating it.

'What are you all up to today? Any plans?' asked Grandma Megan, as she cleaned Cyan's face.

'Well James, and I, thought we'd like to spend the day in Brighton,' said Adele. 'Would you like to come with us Rosie?'

'Thank you, but no. I must do some more studying with Juniper. I have a feeling that whatever I learn will be very useful in the not too distant future.' She smiled at her parents in turn, and they nodded their agreement.

Rosie was sitting fingering the pendant hanging on a chain around her neck. Her mother had recently given it to her for her twelfth birthday. She watched Bella walk in the door from the back garden where she had been supervising Amber.

I wonder, thought Rosie, and she stared at her little dog. She telepathically asked her if she had enjoyed herself outside.

Bella turned to look at Rosie, sat down on the floor and answered, *Yes, thank you, I've had a lovely time.* Bella then sat up on her hind legs, gave one of her beautiful smiles and waved her paws in the air.

Rosie clapped and giggled but only she and Bella knew why. The rest of the family thought it was because Bella was smiling and waving.

'When you have finished your breakfast dear, I'll take you and James, to the station in Marissa in time to catch the Brighton train,' said Grandma Megan. Then I must finish getting the elixir ready for tonight. I think Cornelius will need a little extra boost this year, and I know just the thing. He's very tired and run down. I think it's because he's been working extra hard with so many of us using his door this summer.'

'Grandma Megan, I think it's going to be another lovely day, but I wouldn't be surprised if we have a storm tonight,' said James.

'I'd better make sure all the animals are in a little earlier, if that's the case. Thank you, James,' then turning she asked, 'Trilby what are you up to?'

'I think I'll stay with Rosie,' the little faery replied.

Rosie inwardly groaned. She loved having Trilby around, but she would much rather concentrate on her studies without her. She knew it was because Trilby didn't want to miss anything, and to be fair she had helped Rosie in the past.

That just leaves you Cyan. I think you can stay here with me today, if that's alright with you?'

Grandma Megan looked across, and saw he had stopped eating long enough to look up at her, nod his head in agreement, and then went back to concentrating on his breakfast.

'I think I'll make a start now, if it's alright with everyone,' said Rosie, rising to her feet. 'Have a good day in Brighton Mother, you too Father, and I'll see you this evening.

Rosie walked across to the dining-room, collected Juniper from his special little hiding place and carried him upstairs.

Trilby was already there waiting for her. 'What are you doing today then?' she asked flying across to make herself comfortable on the rocking chair.

'I don't know yet, but I'm sure Juniper will have something in mind,' answered Rosie.

Making herself comfortable on her bed she opened the front cover and wished the old book a good morning.

Trilby watched closely. Because Rosie spoke telepathically with the book, she didn't know what was being said between them any now. Trilby could speak to and understand animals, but the book was a different thing altogether.

Good morning to you Rosie, answered Juniper. *What would you like to know today?*
I don't know, have you any ideas? Rosie asked.
Have you heard of shape shifting Rosie?
No, what's that?
It is to physically transform into another being or form.
That's not possible.
Oh yes, it is, and if you put your mind to it, you are gifted enough to do it. It might come in handy one day. You can change into anything you want to be,
Anything?
Yes, I wouldn't be telling you otherwise. Would you like to try it?
Oh yes, this could be fun.
Good, now make yourself comfortable, and close your eyes, instructed Juniper.

Rosie re-positioned herself and closed her eyes as instructed.

Trilby sat forward knowing something was about to happen, and didn't want to miss anything.

Now, think of a small mammal you would like to be. We'll try that first, not too small mind.
Alright, I'm thinking of a weasel.
Yes, I can see you are.
You can?
We are so closely connected now Rosie, I know what you are thinking.

'Wow,' she breathed.

'What? What?' Trilby asked excitedly.

Rosie ignored her.

Now, continued Juniper, *imagine you are as small as a weasel, covered in fur and that you are that weasel. Relax as much as you can Rosie, and go with it. It will take a little time because this is your first try.*

Rosie inhaled deeply, and slowly exhaled. She now felt very relaxed and was imagining she was a weasel.

After about thirty minutes Trilby was getting bored and fidgety. 'This is taking ages,' he mumbled. 'Whatever is supposed to be happening? I wonder if she has fallen asleep.'

Rosie was concentrating very hard imagining she was a weasel. She then had the strangest feeling something was happening, but wasn't sure, so she continued what she was doing, and kept her eyes closed.

'Yikes!' she heard Trilby scream. The little faery flew off the chair and on to the bed.

Juniper chuckled, then said, *I think it worked then, from what I can hear.*

'Rosie, are you still there?' whispered Trilby.

'What are you talking about?' asked Rosie, opening her eyes. 'Ooohhh, you've grown Trilby,' said Rosie, amazed.

'No, I haven't, you've shrunk.' Trilby replied indignantly. 'You are also covered in fur and have four legs.'

'Really?'

Rosie untangled herself from the clothes she had been wearing and jumping off the bed, ran across the floor to her dressing-table, climbed up and examined herself in the mirror.

'Juniper how long will I stay like this,' Rosie asked in her usual voice.

However long as you wish. You just imagine yourself back to the original Rosie, and you will change back immediately, he advised.

'Back in a minute, I must show Grandma Megan this,' said Rosie, and she climbed down from the dressing-table, ran to the bedroom door, along the landing heading for the stairs.

'Rosie wait,' called Trilby. 'Let me go first and warn Grandma Megan.'

'Alright, but hurry. I'm not sure how long I can stay like this.

'*What!*' Rosie heard her grandma shriek, and knew it was now time to head towards the kitchen. Running into the room she headed for the nearest chair, climbed up, sat on her hind legs, then jumped up onto the table. Grandma Megan was sitting at the table staring at her.

'Rosie?' she asked in a tremulous voice.

'Hello Grandma,' Rosie giggled.

Cyan choked and fell off his chair backwards. Bella lay down and whined, covering and uncovering her eyes, not knowing what to do.

'This is amazing. You can still talk too,' whispered Grandma Megan.

'Well I am still Rosie, it's only my appearance that's changed.'

'You still have your green eyes though. Your powers are getting very strong so fast Rosie. It seems there won't be anything you can't do shortly. Please change back Rosie,' asked Grandma Megan. 'I need a little time to get used to this.'

Rosie climbed back down off the kitchen table, and looking back over her shoulder said to Grandma Megan, 'Would you mind bringing that blanket over to me from the back of the chair. Once I change back I won't have any clothes on, mine are still up in my bedroom.'

Grandma Megan carried the blanket across to Rosie and shook it out holding it out in front of her.

Visualizing herself as the twelve-year-old girl she really was, Rosie slowly grew taller, changing in appearance all the time until she was back to normal. Standing there smiling at her grandma, Rosie asked, 'Are you alright Grandma?'

'Yes dear, I'm fine. Time for a cup of tea I think,' and wrapping the blanket around Rosie, went to fill the kettle and put it on to boil. 'I'll turn into a packet of tea soon, if I carry on drinking so much,' she muttered.

She'll be fine, thought Rosie, and she turned and made her way back up the stairs.

Back in her bedroom she sat down and said to Juniper, *That, was amazing. Frightened the life out of Grandma Megan I think.*

Juniper chuckled. *The more you practice the easier and quicker you will transform. It might come in handy one day, and you will need to be able to do so many different things in the future, and as you get older. Most elves only have one maybe two special powers, but you will have them all, in time.*

Why is that, and how many will I be able to do?

Juniper wasn't going to say any more on the subject now thinking Rosie had enough to think about for the time being. All he said was, *I think you have had enough for today. I suggest you go outside and get some sunshine. Practice running faster if you want something constructive to do.*

Alright, agreed Rosie, and began dressing.

She was feeling a little weary now and hungry too. It must be nearly lunchtime. Saying goodbye to Juniper she closed the old book of magic, carried him downstairs and put him away safely.

Trilby was still in the kitchen when she entered the room.

Are you sure you're alright Grandma?' asked Rosie.

'Right as rain dear, thank you. Funny old saying that isn't it. I really must stop being so surprised at the odd happenings nowadays, don't I? There will be lots more to come I shouldn't wonder. Would you like something to eat and drink?'

'Yes please, I'd love some cheese,' said Rosie.

'Grandma Megan chuckled, then said 'It's a good job you didn't change into a mouse, I would worry you hadn't changed back properly.' They both burst out laughing and started to set the table for lunch,

Trilby wasn't sure what they were laughing about.

193

Chapter 35

Later that same day, Grandma Megan set off in Marissa to collect Adele, and James, from the railway station. She had left Rosie in the barn finishing getting the stables ready for the night.

It did now look as if it was going to be stormy, and as soon as Grandma Megan, Adele, and James, returned home, they would all set to and bring all the animals in to safety.

Grandma Megan had left a large vegetable casserole cooking in the oven. Once the chores were completed they would all sit down together, and enjoy a nice hot meal then wait for when it was time to go and visit Cornelius.

Bertrum, and Wolfric, would be there to meet them at ten thirty.

Singing to herself, Rosie made her way out of the barn carrying an empty bucket. She walked across the yard to the outside tap, and started to fill it with water.

She stopped singing abruptly and looked around her. She felt the same sensation she had felt at the funfair. She was being watched, she was sure of it, and it wasn't a very nice feeling.

Trying to carry on as if she hadn't noticed anything odd, she carried the now full bucket back to the barn and emptied it into Hector's large water container in the corner of his stable.

Thankful everything was now ready for the animals, Rosie headed back across the yard and entered the cottage.

Hello Bella, would you, and Amber, like your dinner a little earlier than usual?

Bella cocked her head on one side, smiled and replied, *Yes, please, that would be great. I get hungry following this little one around all day.*

This is wonderful being able to talk to you like I always have in the past Bella, but now being able to understand your answers telepathically is extra special.

Rosie picked up the two bowls of food and carried them across to Bella's basket and placed them on the floor. Young Amber came scampering across the floor but didn't stop in time at her bowl, and dived in head first.

Sneezing a couple of times, she recovered sufficiently to start eating.

'Enthusiastic about everything isn't she,' remarked Rosie.

Bella just grinned, and started tucking into her own dinner.

Standing there watching them both, Trilby then flew in the door very agitated. 'Rosie, Rosie, you have to be very careful,' she warned.

'Calm down Trilby. What's the matter?'

'Well, I was sitting up in a tree by the bridge, when I noticed two strangers creeping towards the homestead. They were moving from tree to tree, and I knew they didn't want to be seen,' said Trilby.

'I had a feeling I was being watched,' replied Rosie. 'What did you do?'

'I went and told Erin. He was sleeping in the barn, and wasn't too pleased to be woken up I can tell you. I told him what I'd seen and he went out and chased them off. You should have seen their faces. Erin stood in front of them, growled showing his teeth, and they couldn't get away fast enough. One of them tripped over and fell into something smelly and nasty,' laughed Trilby.

'Thank you, Trilby. What would I do without you now,' praised Rosie. 'We'll mention this to the others at dinner.'

**

That evening, after they had all enjoyed Grandma Megan's casserole, with spotted dick and custard for pudding, they sat relaxed and talking about the events of the day.

Rosie turned to the little faery and said, 'I think now is the time to let everyone know what you saw Trilby.'

Trilby flew onto the table and stood importantly in the centre, so she could turn and look at everyone whilst relaying what she had seen.

'This is very serious,' said Avery. 'They can't be after James again surely.'

'No, I don't think so. They seemed to be intent on Rosie,' said Trilby.

'We need to make sure you're never left here on your own in the future Rosie,' said Grandma Megan. 'You'll be coming with us tonight anyway, but as Adele, and James, will be in the cottage when we go to Cornelius, I'll ask Erin if he would mind guarding the cottage until we return.'

'Good idea.' agreed Avery. 'I'll have a word with Bertrum tonight, and ask if he's managed to get any information out of those two thugs they have locked up there.'

'Listen to that weather outside. You were right James, I'm glad we fetched all the animals in,' said Grandma Megan. 'I hope it eases off in time for us to go out. We'll get soaked to the skin otherwise.'

Everyone then pitched in and helped to clear the table, wash up and put everything away.

It was almost time for Grandma Megan, Rosie and Avery to leave the cottage, and make their way to Cornelius.

Avery quickly put on his mackintosh, and nipped across to the barn to have a word with Erin. Erin was only too pleased to help and trotted alongside Avery back to the cottage. He wasn't planning on going out tonight in this weather anyway,

Grandma Megan, and Rosie, were ready and waiting to go when he arrived back in the cottage,

'All set?' enquired Grandma Megan.

'Ready,' chorused Rosie, and Avery.

They said their goodbyes to Adele, James, and Erin, and closing the cottage door behind them hurried down to the gate, then made their way across the field towards the forest as fast as they could.

Arriving in the glade, they expected to see Cornelius, Bertrum and Wolfric, waiting for them, but they were nowhere in sight.

Sheltering as much as they could under the trees, Avery said in a low voice, 'I hope everything is alright and we don't have to wait too long. It's not like Bertrum to be late.'

They waited another ten long minutes, and then saw Cornelius start to materialize, but then he was gone again.

'Something's very wrong,' whispered Grandma Megan.

Rosie was standing close beside her grandma biting her lip. They were all soaking wet and the weather didn't seem to be getting any better.

Another few long minutes passed, and then Cornelius was there in the glade.

'Quick everyone, run as fast as you can,' urged Avery.

Just as they reached the great old oak, the little door opened and Bertrum, and Wolfric stepped out. The little door closed again.

Grandma Megan reached into her pockets and pulled out the little silver cup from one, and the bottle of elixir from the other.

'He is so weak now, I'm not sure how long we have Megan, so speed is of the essence,' said Bertrum. 'He is only just holding on.'

'I forgot to bring the ladder,' gasped Avery.

Jaws dropped as they all stared at him.

Cornelius's mouth was too high up for any one person to reach. Grandma Megan usually climbed up the ladder and administered the potion, but that was out of the question now.

'There's only one thing for it,' said Bertrum. 'Avery, you are the tallest, and Rosie here is the lightest in weight. Her powers are getting stronger too so that will also help Cornelius.'

'What!' squeaked Rosie, as Bertrum nodded at Grandma Megan, asking for her approval? She nodded back, took the stopper out of the bottle and filled the little silver cup.

Avery clasped one of Rosie's hands and pulled her across to stand with him under the face of Cornelius. He bent down and with the help of Bertrum, and Wolfric, Rosie climbed onto Avery's shoulders.

Avery stood up straight close to the front of the tree, for which Rosie was grateful, because she could stretch out an arm and place a hand on the tree's bark to steady herself.

'Rosie take the cup,' instructed Grandma Megan. 'Try not to spill any. He needs every drop.'

Rosie leaned down and took the cup with her other hand then slowly stood up straight. She was just under the mouth of Cornelius.

'What do I do now?' she asked trying not to wobble and drop the cup. She couldn't figure out where to pour the liquid.

'Brace yourself against the tree dear, and tap his lower lip. That will register with him to open his mouth, and you can empty all the contents into it,' instructed Grandma Megan.

Concentrating hard, Rosie did as she was told and very slowly Cornelius opened his mouth just enough to receive the potion. Carefully Rosie poured every drop into his mouth, gently shaking the cup to make sure it was empty.

'Well done Rosie,' praised Wolfric, giving a little dance.

Rosie watched intently, but she couldn't see any change happening.

'Catch the cup,' she called, and she carefully dropped it into waiting hands.

The cup, now safely back in Bertrum's pocket ready to be taken back to Oakenveil,

Rosie turned back to Cornelius, and placed her hands over as much of the tree's face as she could reach.

'What's she doing?' asked Avery, not being able to see with Rosie standing on his shoulders.

'I think Rosie is using her healing hands,' whispered Grandma Megan.

'Clever girl,' praised Avery.

'Better hold her legs tight,' said Grandma Megan.

It was a good thing Grandma Megan had advised Avery to hold tight to Rosie's legs because if she hadn't, Rosie would have toppled off his shoulders backwards.

Cornelius suddenly opened his eyes wide and a big smile lit up his face.

Taken by surprise, Rosie leaned backwards.

'Get her down quickly,' urged Grandma Megan. She had seen this happen once before and it might be too much for young Rosie, being so close. Bertrum, and Wolfric, lifted Rosie down off Avery's shoulders, and they all moved away from the tree.

Cornelius was starting to glow. From the top of his branches, down to the tips of his roots the glow spread, and he emitted such a powerful pulse that it lit up the entire glade.

'I haven't seen that happen before,' gasped Bertrum. 'What did you put in the elixir Megan?'

'Love, Bertrum, lots of love.'

'Powerful stuff.'

'It is. That and Rosie's healing hands, did the trick,' said Grandma Megan.

All of them now had huge smiles on their faces standing there watching Cornelius.

The glow was starting to fade now, and Cornelius was returning to normal.

'Oh dear,' groaned Wolfric.

The rest turned to look at him wondering what was wrong.

'Follow me, quickly,' he whispered and he turned and made his way into the forest. Out of sight of Cornelius he turned and said, 'That warden chap was standing watching.'

'I didn't think he'd be out this late or in this weather,' said Grandma Megan. 'What are we to do?' she asked anxiously.

'I have an idea,' said Rosie. 'You all wait here.'

Rosie went behind a large tree nearby and concentrated hard. Before too long her clothes dropped to the ground and she was running towards Fred Bennett. Fred was still standing on the edge of the glade, watching Cornelius not believing his eyes.

He was in for another shock. Rosie reached Fred, stood up on her hind legs and spoke to him. He was so engrossed watching Cornelius glowing, that Rosie had to tug on his trouser leg to get his attention.

Absentmindedly, Fred glanced down and then staggered back a couple of paces. What he saw was a very dry weasel looking up at him. It was just too much for Fred when the weasel spoke to him and said, 'Hello Fred, do you know Jack the gypsy boy is setting traps only a few hundred yards away over there.'

Fred's eyes fluttered, and he fell backwards in a dead feint.

That should keep him out of the way for enough time for us to finish our task, thought Rosie, and she scampered back to the tree, changed back into her normal self and re-dressed.

'How long has she been doing that?' enquired Wolfric.

'Oh, not long at all,' laughed Grandma Megan. 'Our Rosie is a quick learner.'

'Splendid!' enthused Avery, who hadn't been informed of this development before either.

Re-joining the others Rosie asked, 'What do we do now? We can't leave poor Fred lying there in the rain all night.'

'Don't worry Rosie, we'll carry him home, and he'll think he's had a weird dream. He will probably come back here early in the morning to check, but we'll make sure there is nothing for him to see,' replied Avery,

'Let's get back to Cornelius,' suggested Bertrum. 'His glow is fading fast so he should be ready to let us back in now and disappear.'

Standing in front of Cornelius, they all thought they had never seen him look so strong and well.

'Hello one and all,' he greeted and winked.

'Glad to see you are looking so much better,' said Grandma Megan.

'Oh, I'm feeling fine now. I expect I have you to thank for the extra boost Grandma Megan,' he replied.

Just then the rain stopped and the new moon shone down on them all, bright and clear.

'We'll say goodnight now. Thank you so much Megan, and you too Rosie, and Avery,' said Bertrum. 'Are you sure you don't want any help with that game warden chap?'

'No, thank you, we'll be fine,' assured Avery.

'Goodnight then, see you in a couple of evenings when we use the rocket,' said Bertrum. 'Come along Wolfric.'

Wolfric wished everyone a goodnight, but before entering the door in the tree he turned, grinned, and said 'I wouldn't have missed this for the world. I can't wait for the rocket launch.' He then stepped through the small door, and Cornelius closed it and disappeared.

'Now for poor Fred. How are we going to get him home?' asked Grandma Megan.

Without a word, Avery walked across to where Fred was still lying on the ground, touched him in the middle of his forehead with the index finger of his right hand and hoisted him up into a fireman's lift.

'What did you just do to him?' asked Rosie.

'Just put him into a peaceful sleep until the morning,' answered Grandma Megan. 'We don't want him waking up halfway home. We'll just leave him in his armchair and he'll think he's fallen asleep after his dinner. His door won't be locked because he's out and about, and I'm sure Ivy will be tucked up in bed asleep.'

'Poor Fred,' said Rosie, feeling sorry for him, but at the same time she couldn't help giggling.

Chapter 36

All was peaceful the next day for a change, and everyone was busy with their various tasks.

Avery was putting the finishing touches to the rocket. He had been to see the local farmer and borrowed his tractor and trailer for a couple of days so he could tow the rocket out to the launching site.

Grandma Megan was attending to her herbs and potions. She also popped into the village to check on Ivy, and she was curious to see if Fred was alright after the night before.

Rosie was still studying, and learning many things from Juniper.

All the animals were behaving themselves and Adele, and James, were enjoying the peace of the countryside before they returned to London. Trilby was happy to just sit in a tree and watch, making sure nothing was amiss.

**

The following evening was bright and clear. Just right for a rocket launch.

Sitting around chatting after the evening meal, they were all enjoying each other's company, and had fun pulling the party crackers Avery had made using the toilet roll cardboard inserts he had been collecting all around the village.

'I wondered what you were collecting these for,' laughed Grandma Megan.

'I have plenty left for the Christmas festivities too, and will put extra little bits and pieces inside for that occasion,' said Avery, enjoying himself.

Adele, and James, would be returning to London the next day and this was their last evening altogether for a while.

'How was Fred when you saw him Megan?' asked James, smiling. Grandma Megan, and Rosie, had told them all about the events of the evening with Cornelius.

'He was fine, I think. I only saw him for a quick word before he went out on his rounds after his lunch, but Ivy told me afterwards, he kept mumbling about a glowing tree and a talking weasel. I suggested to her that maybe he was working too hard, and she ought to try and keep him home tonight for a rest. Whether she will have any luck with that, I don't know.'

Avery stood up and made his way to the door. 'Nearly time to leave,' he said. 'I'll just check over a few things, and then we should go.'

The tractor was already hitched to the large trailer, and the rocket was strapped down tight so it didn't move on the journey. Avery was anxious to get it to the launching site, prepared the day before, before the light faded.

Grandma Megan, Rosie, and Adele, were staying at the cottage so it was James, who accompanied Avery.

Bertrum, Wolfric, and a few of the other elves would be bringing Lanky Lance, and Beaky, to the launching site.

Avery, and James, climbed onto the tractor. Avery started it up, and they were off.

Driving very slowly making nothing went amiss, they eventually arrived. Avery drove the tractor right up to the launching site making sure the trailer was right beside the prepared launching pad. He switched off the tractor, and they both jumped down after Avery applied the brake.

Quickly untying the straps securing the rocket, James turned to Avery with a puzzled expression and asked, 'How are you going to get this huge thing off the trailer and standing upright?'

Avery smiled and said, 'You'll see in a minute. Stand over here just behind me if you will.'

James did so and to say he was astonished at what he was witnessing, was putting it mildly.

Avery was standing a few feet away from the trailer and he slowly started to raise his arms into the air. The rocket began to lift off the trailer. Once it was high enough to clear the sides of the trailer he adjusted the position of his hands and with a pushing motion the rocket floated towards the launching pad and hovered over it. He then raised his arms high so the rocket rose higher so when tilted and the nose pointed up in the air, the legs of the rocket were in the right position to slot into the stabilizers when it was lowered.

Satisfied it was in the right position Avery put his arms down and strode across to make sure all was well, and the rocket steady.

'I didn't know you could do that,' said James,' very impressed.

'No reason why you should,' replied Avery, smiling. 'I don't get to use it very often, but every now and again it comes in handy.'

Avery then drove the tractor and trailer a safe distance away, so nothing would happen to it once the rocket launched.

They didn't have to wait very long after that. Bertrum, Wolfric, and the other elves were now approaching.

Lanky Lance, and Beaky, had their hands tied behind their backs and both were blindfolded. They were being unceremoniously marched across the field, and the two were stumbling and tripping over parts of the ground that were uneven. The elves didn't have any pity for the two thugs, and just yanked them to their feet and carried on.

Avery stepped over to the rocket, and opened the door ready.

Lanky Lance was the first to arrive, and he was helped up the steps into the top seat. He was securely strapped in before the blindfold was removed and his hands untied.

'Where am I?' he demanded.

Nobody answered him.

Next it was Beaky's turn, and he was strapped into the seat underneath Lanky Lance. His blindfold and ties were also removed.

'What's going on?' demanded Beaky.

'If you were expecting to be rescued on your journey to Elmsville, where you will spend the next thirty years in the prison there, you are going to be sadly disappointed,' said Bertrum.

'Don't know what you are talking about,' said Lanky Lance, full of bravado.

'In case you haven't noticed yet, you are strapped into a rocket which will take you straight to your journey's end,' informed Bertrum.

He then signalled to Avery to close and lock the door. As they all retreated to a safe distance they could all clearly hear the two inside the rocket, shouting and swearing.

'I just couldn't resist telling them,' gloated Bertrum. 'Their bravado soon disappeared, didn't it?'

Avery picked up a little black box from the tractor seat, and looking at the others asked 'Ready?'

They all nodded in unison.

Avery flipped a black switch, and then pressed a large red button. The engine started with such force and began burning the fuel. This then generated a lot of heat producing gas. The build-up of gas escaping the rocket was extremely loud, and all but Avery had very worried expressions on their faces. He just stood there nodding his head in approval.

The force of the escaping gas provided enough thrust to power the rocket upwards, and before too long it was lifting off the ground, and heading for the sky.

'How will they come down?' asked one of the elves.

'I've worked out the distance to Elmsville, and the rocket has enough fuel to get there and no further. It will fall into the large lake near the village. I hope you have asked the elves over at Elmsville to be ready and waiting to fish them out, when they splash down,' said Avery, turning to Bertrum.

Bertrum laughed, and confirmed he had been in touch with them that morning, and everything was arranged

'Did you manage to get any information out of either of those two as to why they had kidnapped James and held him so long?' asked Avery.

'Yes, we did,' replied Bertrum. Beaky, the small tubby one, sang like a little bird when he thought he would get a lighter sentence if he talked. That didn't happen.'

'So, what did he say?'

'You are all going to have to be extra vigilant in the future Avery. Apparently, there is a large gathering of dark witches, over near Elmsville, and the high priestess is determined to get her hands on the old book of magic.'

'But she won't know how to use it surely,' said Avery, aghast.

'I don't know whether she has the means to do so or not, but we must never give her the opportunity to try. That is why she is sending out scouts to find the book, and it was too good an opportunity to miss when they came across James, and kidnapped him. They thought, if they held on to him, until Rosie came of age and received the book, we would hand the book over to get James back. You and I know it has been well hidden for years until now. If by any means this high priestess does get her hands on the book, she will be all powerful. Also, if she captures Rosie, I hate to think what might happen to her especially if this high priestess discovers how powerful Rosie is becoming, and wants to make use of her.

'Isn't there anything extra we can do to protect her?'

'Make sure she always has someone with her, even if it's only Trilby. Trilby has proved herself lately, and I know you can trust her now. We can arrange for protection spells to surround her also. But Rosie must be told so she can be on her guard.'

'Poor Rosie,' moaned Avery. 'So much is happening to her lately. She is still such a young girl.'

'I know, but better to be on our guard now than sorry later. I think you will find Rosie is stronger and braver than you give her credit for.'

They each then said goodnight, and the elves headed back towards Cornelius and their village.

Avery, and James, got onto the tractor and made their way back to the cottage. It would be late when they returned and stored the tractor and trailer, so they decided to tell Grandma Megan and the others what they had found out in the morning.

Jack the gypsy boy was the only one to see the rocket flying over the forest that night. He was busy setting rabbit traps, and thought when he heard the loud engine, it was a low flying aircraft or maybe one in trouble, but when he looked up to a break in the canopy of trees he was astonished to see the rocket.

I think I'll keep this to myself, he thought. Nobody would believe me anyway. Why would there be a rocket flying around here?

Chapter 37

The next morning dawned bright and clear. Another beautiful summer's day. Who would ever imagine that evil would be lurking, thought Avery, as he made his way from his workshop cum living quarters up to the cottage to join the others for breakfast.

Adele and James were planning on returning to London today, but whether they would still go after hearing what he had to tell them all, he didn't know.

After they had all eaten their breakfast, Avery told them all about the rocket launch, and how it had been a great success.

'Did Bertrum learn any more about why they had kidnapped and held James for so long?' asked Grandma Megan.

'Yes, he did.'

'Well?'

'There's a large coven gathering over the other side of Elmsville, and the high priestess of that coven is determined to get Juniper. She will then have control over all of us, elves, faeries, villages, everything. She is powerful in her own right, but with the old book of magic, well it doesn't bear thinking about.'

Avery took a long drink of orange juice. He wasn't one for talking very much generally, and now his mouth was very dry from relaying all the facts, and with fear.

'Adele, turned to James, and said, 'Maybe we shouldn't return to London today.'

Before he could reply, Grandma Megan spoke and said, 'I think you should go. I know you don't want to and are worried about Rosie and the rest of us, but I think both you, and James, will be safer there with so many people about.

London is a very busy place, and we don't want you, or James, in any more danger down here. James has been through enough already.

'But…,' began Adele.

'Now, no buts,' cut in Grandma Megan. 'I will take you both to the station in Marissa after breakfast to catch the London train. Don't worry, we'll be fine and we'll all watch out for each other here.'

'That's probably sensible,' agreed Avery.

Rosie was sitting very still not saying a word, but she was looking very pale.

Trilby flew across, sat on her shoulder and whispered into Rosie's ear, 'It'll be alright, you'll see.'

Rosie gave a little nod of her head, hoping the little faery was right.

After more discussion, it was decided that Adele, and James, would return to London. Adele would resume her work at the large hospital, and James would ask if he could work in the university he'd travelled the world for, instead of taking trips abroad. For the time being anyway.

There was a knock on the back door which made everyone jump out of their skins.

'Whoever can that be,' said Grandma Megan, rising from her chair at the table to go and see.

They all sat very still, watching and waiting.

'Morning everyone,' greeted Wolfric, as he breezed into the kitchen, a big grin on his face.

'Wolfric,' gasped Rosie, but she was very pleased to see him. 'What are you doing here?'

'I persuaded my father that I might be more use here instead of just sitting around at home.'

'What a good idea,' agreed Grandma Megan. 'You're very welcome dear. Sit down and have some juice or something and talk to Rosie. I'm just about to take Adele, and James, to the station.

Satisfied Rosie wasn't going to be left on her own, Avery said his farewells to Adele, and James, and headed off down to his workshop.

'I expect you know what's going on,' Rosie said to Wolfric,

'Yes, I was there last night when my father told Avery,' he replied.

'It's all a bit scary, isn't it?' said Rosie, looking at the young elf.

'Oh, I don't know,' he replied. 'Things used to be very quiet and a bit boring before you came, but now it seems like one adventure after another. It's great!'

Rosie was starting to feel a little better, and was glad Wolfric was with them.

'Hello Trilby,' Wolfric greeted the little faery. 'Been up to any mischief lately?'

'I don't do mischief any more,' she replied haughtily, and flew off to see what was going on outside.

Adele, and James, entered the kitchen carrying their cases and put them down onto the kitchen floor.

'Are you sure you want to stay here with Grandma Megan?' Adele asked her daughter. 'You know you can come back with us if you want to, now or at any time in the future.'

'No, thank you, I'd rather stay here. I'll be starting at the village school soon, which I'm quite looking forward to. I'd hate to return to that London school.'

'Alright darling, if you're sure.'

'Yes, I am.'

'Are you coming to the station with us,' enquired James.

'I'd rather say goodbye here,' said Rosie.

Adele stretched out her arms, and Rosie stood up and went to give her mother and her father big hugs. Then walking with them to the door Rosie watched as Grandma Megan took Adele's case, and carried it out to the car placing it in the boot.

Grandma Megan, Adele, and James, got into Marissa.

Grandma Megan started the little car and they slowly started down the lane.

But what would the future hold? Both parents couldn't help wondering, and worrying, as they set off on their journey back to London. Adele, and James, both turned looking out of the rear window of Marissa, until Rosie disappeared.

TO BE CONTINUED

If you enjoyed this second book in the trilogy it would be much appreciated if you would take the time to leave a review and check out Lee's catalogue

Catalogue of Lee Marsh's Books

The Magic Within – The Dawning

The Magic Within – Triple Quest

The Magic Within – Deception

Mirimuss The Forgetful Wizard

Printed in Great Britain
by Amazon